DEADLY STILL

Inspector Torquil McKinnon Mystery Book Six

Keith Moray

SAPERE
BOOKS

Also in the Torquil McKinnon Mystery Series

The Gathering Murders

Deathly Wind

Murder Solstice

Flotsam & Jetsam

Death in Transit

DEADLY STILL

Published by Sapere Books.

20 Windermere Drive, Leeds, England, LS17 7UZ,
United Kingdom

saperebooks.com

ISBN: 978-1-913335-39-7

Keith Moray is represented by Isabel Atherton at Creative
Authors.

In memory of my grandfather, an experienced head maltman at several Speyside distilleries, who taught me how to spin a yarn. Also in memory of my mother, who was born in a distillery cottage and who was convinced that she had whisky in her blood. Consequently, she never had a desire to take a dram.

Uisge beatha
Chan uisge beatha ach uisge bais

Translation:
Whisky (the water of life)
It is not the water of life but the water of death

PROLOGUE

The killer looked down at the body with a critical eye. Something wasn't quite right about the way it would look to someone discovering it. The position of the legs would look too contrived.

I can't risk that. It needs to look natural, as if there had been a sudden seizure and the body slumped forward and fell flat on its face. That would be in keeping, for everyone knows how much the bastard drinks at nights. I'll reposition them afterwards.

The killer lifted the head by the hair and the torso by the collar until it was raised as far as the spine would allow. Then, placing a foot on the back of the neck and stamping down hard at the same time as letting go with the hands, the head was forcibly driven onto the bare wooden floor. A sickening thud ensued and a crunch as the nasal bones shattered. A pool of blood immediately started to form around the head.

Gingerly lifting the whisky glass in a gloved hand and holding it above and to the side of the body the slayer threw it at a slight angle so that it smashed and splashed its contents forwards. For added effect the empty whisky bottle was rolled across the floor, sloshing liquid as it went until it stopped against the skirting board.

Good, a masterful touch there. It looks as if the glass fell forward out of one hand and the bottle out of the other. A waste of good whisky, they'll say! OK, maybe not good whisky, but that's for them to find out.

At least I didn't spit in your face, like you deserved, but I'm not going to risk leaving any of my DNA around this place. Not when I was so careful to wear gloves as always in this pigsty. Not that there will be a need for anyone to even look for such ephemera when the cause of death is so obvious, you drunken sot.

If you were still alive you'd realise it was all your own fault. If you hadn't been such a greedy bastard and forced my hand you'd still be leading your dirty little life and you'd be able to keep your murky secrets to yourself. Lucky for your legacy, if there was such a thing, I'm here to clear your crap up for you.

The killer picked up the phone and carefully checked that there were no photos in the phone library before tossing it onto the kitchen table beside the bottles of insulin and the used syringe.

It all went according to my plan, even though you thought you were in charge. The drink did the trick and then a huge insulin dose made sure, so all I had to do was slip the tube up your nostril and down into the stomach and pour the contents of a whole bottle into it via the feeding bag.

I expected that there would be some vomiting, a gag reflex I suppose, but that little bit of gubbins on your clothes makes it look even better. That fit you had was spectacular, especially with all that frothy spittle. Another nice touch that they'll put down to a seizure while pissed out of your head.

Beautiful! Untraceable! Just bad whisky, they'll think. If they think at all! And now with that smashed nose there is no trace of where I shoved the tube. So it's goodbye then, you fucking toad. I'm glad I had the pleasure of snuffing your miserable life out.

The killer put the nasogastric tube and the feeding bag in the plastic rubbish bag along with the laptop and the other potentially incriminating things that had been carefully stowed there.

Taking out the mobile phone the killer sent a quick one-word text before spending a few minutes minutely removing all possible traces from the other room. Then, after one last look around to check that no traces had been left, opened the door and slipped out into the night.

CHAPTER ONE

Sergeant Morag Driscoll's first thought on waking had been to roll over and enjoy the fact that her schoolteacher sister, who taught at Oban High School on the mainland, had kindly taken Morag's three children along with her own on holiday to Majorca. Instead, guilt kicked in and she threw herself out of bed, had a cup of tea and a dry cracker and then went for a jog in the early morning mist.

Morag was a thirty-something single mother of three, whose husband had died from a heart attack when he was only thirty-five and she was just twenty-six. From that day she vowed that she would always be there for her children. She watched her diet and she kept as fit as possible.

As she made herself pick up her pace on the track parallel with the coast she reflected on how good her life was. Her kids were doing well at school, she couldn't have been happier in her work and her relationship with Sandy King, the Scottish international footballer, was growing deeper and more meaningful with every day. The only problem was that his football career was demanding and they had to grasp whatever time together that they could, especially during the playing season.

Bloody game, she thought to herself with a smile. *Why couldn't I fall in love with a fisherman or a farmer, or at least a local amateur footballer?*

She selected one of the many sheep tracks through the heather and made for the headland trail towards the old Second World War pillbox atop Harpoon Hill, which overlooked the shingle beach of Whaler's Bay some fifty feet below. Although there had never been a whaling station on West Uist, back at the turn of the twentieth-century a Norwegian, Karl Herlofsen and his family ran a whaling station at Bun Abhainn Eadarra on the Isle of Harris. A fleet of catcher vessels worked out of there and harpooned whales at sea and took them to places like Village Bay on St Kilda, Rockall and the Flannan Isles and Whaler's Bay on West Uist. There the whales were secured before being towed back for processing at the Bun Abhainn Eadarra station.

During World War II, because Whaler's Bay was a reasonably protected anchorage, a series of anti-tank concrete blocks had been installed along its length and, since Harpoon Hill above it was a natural vantage point, a pillbox was built on top.

The ground was muddy in patches where it never completely dried out and she knew from bitter experience to beware the many rabbit excavated holes that awaited a careless walker or runner, especially in the mist or fog that concealed so much.

The track zigzagged upwards towards Harpoon Hill. Morag was pacing herself going up the incline and when she was about fifty metres away she heard someone groaning. It sounded to be coming from the pillbox. She distinctly heard a young female voice cursing loudly. Then the screaming started.

Morag stopped to catch her breath and look up at the pillbox to assess the situation. Someone was definitely screaming. It sounded like a young woman's, high-pitched and prolonged, as if in abject terror.

What the devil, she thought. Surely it couldn't be real, not out here this early on such a foggy morning. It must be youngsters playing around, trying to startle the runner they'd been watching coming up the hill. She half expected them to come running out any minute once they recognised her.

The pillbox had been a place that bored or rebellious teenagers would hang out on occasions and drink themselves stupid with cider. Morag knew that from her own teenage years. *I'll give whoever sold them cider what for*, she promised herself as she continued to jog upwards towards the pillbox.

Suddenly, the figure of a young woman — a purple-haired teenager dressed in a baggy pullover, jeans and wellies — staggered out of the pillbox. She looked drunk, very drunk. Alarmingly though, she was screaming hysterically and rubbing her eyes as she stumbled about. Morag recognised her. It was Catriona McDonald, the local councillor's daughter.

'Catriona!' Morag called out, all too aware that she was breathing heavily after the uphill run. 'It's me, Sergeant Driscoll. Settle yourself. Don't move any further, it's really foggy and you're near the edge of the cliff. I'm coming for you.'

The girl did not settle, but instead continued to scream. She lowered her hands from her eyes and held them out fully stretched as if trying to touch something.

'Wh-who's there?' Catriona stammered. She was blinking rapidly and her face was contorted with fear. 'I … I can't see!'

Morag reached her and put a comforting hand on each upper arm. 'It's me, Catriona. Sergeant Morag Driscoll. I've got you. Have you been drinking in the pillbox? You're cold and trembling — have you been in there all night? Is anyone in there with you?'

The girl was shaking frantically. Her screaming had stopped when Morag held her, only to be replaced by uncontrollable sobbing.

Goodness, she reeks of booze, Morag thought.

'J-Jamie Mackintosh and V-Vicky Spiers. Bu-but, I canna wake Jamie.'

'Have you just woken up, Catriona?'

The girl nodded as she continued to sob loudly.

'So Jamie is inside? What about Vicky?'

With difficulty, Catriona replied, 'He's there. I-I felt him, but I can't see… It's just mist and sparks in my eyes.'

Morag bent down to look into the teenager's eyes and felt real worry for her. She was staring straight at her, but there was no pupillary reaction. It was like looking at a doll's eyes.

I am not liking this at all, Morag thought. *I need to get help, but first I need to check on Jamie and Vicky.* She gave Catriona's arms a reassuring squeeze. 'I have to check on the other two, Catriona. Just stay right here. OK?'

The girl nodded and continued to shiver and sob.

It was dark inside the pillbox and Morag saw that the teenagers had stuck cardboard over the viewing window slits. On the floor she found a LED camping lantern and switched it on. By its light she saw Jamie Mackintosh lying on his back, half covered in a blanket. There was frothy spittle on his lips that had solidified as it had trailed down his chin. Alarmingly, his eyes were wide open and in the light from the lantern the pupils seemed totally dilated.

There was no one else in the pillbox.

Training prevented panic and Morag searched for a pulse at his wrist and then at his neck. She couldn't feel one and he was totally unresponsive as she shook him. She listened for breathing and cleared the spittle away before opening his mouth and making sure there was nothing obstructing his breathing.

'Jamie! Jamie! Can you hear me?' she asked, knowing already that he could not. Rushing outside she pulled out her phone from her runner's pouch bag, only to find that it was dead. She suppressed the curse that rose to her lips. 'Catriona, have you got a phone?'

'No. V-Vicky has one. Jamie's ran out last night. Oh Sergeant … I can't see. What's happened. I feel so, so…' She suddenly bent down and vomited.

Pausing only long enough to make sure the youngster wasn't going to faint Morag placed an arm about her shoulders. 'Catriona, I have to see what I can do for Jamie. You're freezing so I'm going to get you a blanket.'

She rushed back inside and picked up one of the blankets that the teenagers had brought with them and took it out to drape around Catriona, who had stopped retching and was on her hands and knees.

'Catriona, listen to me. This is important. I have to see if I can revive Jamie. If you hear a vehicle call me straight away.'

Morag dashed back inside and began cardio-pulmonary resuscitation on the teenager, albeit with little hope of success.

God, please send someone to help, she silently prayed to herself as she began chest compressions. Her last CPR course had been only a month before and Doctor McLelland, the CPR instructor, had given them all tunes that they could use in their heads to get the right rhythm. Working on a plastic dummy humming the Bee Gee's 'Staying Alive' or Queen's 'Another One Bites the Dust' had seemed vaguely amusing at the time. But now, with a teenager that she had known since he was a toddler, she disliked the idea intensely. He was a human being and she needed to do her utmost for him.

She counted thirty compressions and then with the back of her hand wiped the encrusted saliva from the teenager's mouth before giving him two rescue breaths mouth to mouth. And then she started again.

She had been working solidly for ten minutes and felt her arms aching when Catriona screamed out her name. She stopped and listened. In the distance she distinctly heard the noise of a vehicle on the nearby road.

'It has to be whisky, Lorna!' Torquil McKinnon, the Detective Inspector of the West Uist Police said emphatically into his mobile phone as he crunched across the gravel drive leading up to the St Ninian's manse and pushed open the front door of the porch. Wisps of mist followed and swirled about him. 'Whisky is traditional at celebrations for the men on West Uist,' he continued. '*Uisge beatha!* The Water of Life! A wee miniature of Glen Corlin would go down a treat with them. It's one of the oldest malt whiskies in the Outer Hebrides.'

'You're not trying to pull rank on me, are you, Detective Inspector McKinnon?' Lorna replied.

Torquil heard the humorous lilt in her voice and could just picture her sitting in her neat, crisp uniform in her open plan office in the Stornoway station, a cup of tea by her side and her desk in meticulous order. He could almost see her smile and he felt goosebumps all over, for he could never resist that smile, whether real or conjured up in his imagination.

Standing inside the porch he shook his head, as if she could see him. 'Of course not, Sergeant Golspie!' he replied jauntily. 'When it comes to the wedding, our marriage and our life away from the force, we are totally equal partners. We always will be.'

'And yet methinks the wedding favours seem to be one of our first bones of contention.'

'Not at all. Look Lorna, if not Glen Corlin maybe we could give them a miniature of Hamish McNab's Abhainn Dhonn? It's not bad for such a young malt and after all it's also distilled in West Uist. And as for the lassies, well everyone loves Kyleshiffin tablet, don't they?'

'Ha! You think so? Look Torquil, not everyone likes whisky. Artisan gin and rum are trendy these days and we could get that locally produced, too. In fact, I know exactly where we could get them. As for tablet and all that sugar for the "lassies" — do you not think that is a bit sexist? Maybe you're being a bit too parochial here?'

'Sexist and parochial, am I?' Torquil spluttered. He pursed his lips and turned to whistle to Crusoe, his tri-coloured collie, who was busy sniffing back and forth among the molehills that dotted the manse lawns.

'Is that you whistling to keep me quiet?' Lorna said in his ear.

'Och no! I was just calling —'

'Crusoe! I deduced that, Torquil. Not bad, eh, what with me not being a detective like you.' The humour in her tone removed any real suggestion of sarcasm. 'Give him a cuddle from me.'

'Of course I will, but listen, Lorna. I'm not sure about —'

'Oh, there's the boss coming in,' she interrupted abruptly. 'I'll need to go. Just promise me you'll think about it. Let's talk when I get back at the end of the week. Love you.'

'Aye and I —'

There was a click and the line went dead.

'— love you, too,' Torquil added wistfully before stowing the phone in a pocket of his jeans. He turned and whistled again to Crusoe. He opened the heavy oak door and stood aside to let him dash past him.

The length of the hall was home to an assortment of carburettor components, oil filters and gears which lay on spread-out oil-stained newspapers. They belonged to a classic Excelsior Talisman motorcycle that he and his uncle had been slowly 'rebuilding' over more years than they cared to remember. In the past they would tinker with them now and then, and talk of how fine it was going to be when they finally completed it and were able to take it out for its maiden trip. Other things had gradually diverted their interest, like golf in his uncle's case and a certain female sergeant in Torquil's, so that now the only real attention the components received was a weekly once-over with a feather duster and an occasional spot of oil so that the illusion of an on-going project was maintained. Even Crusoe had ceased to be intrigued by the engine smells and ignored them as he bounded round the corner.

The mouth-watering aroma of grilled bacon, black pudding and toast wafted through from the kitchen and Torquil hung up Crusoe's lead on the ancient umbrella stand and followed the dog through.

His uncle, the Reverend Lachlan McKinnon, known throughout West Uist as the Padre, stood at the Aga stirring a pan of scrambled eggs with one hand while he read a golf magazine with the other.

'Morning, laddie. I've got it all ready. A good breakfast is what you need before a hard day's toil. Look at Crusoe, he's straight into his.'

Torquil cast a glance at Crusoe who was noisily eating from his bowl in the corner of the kitchen. He smiled, then went over to the old enamel sink and washed his hands. 'I must say that I haven't much enthusiasm for work this morning, Uncle,' he said as he sat down and unrolled his napkin.

There was an obvious resemblance between the two men. Both were tall and had the same slightly hawk-like features. Torquil had been the youngest ever inspector in the Hebridean Constabulary, before it was absorbed into the modern national

Police Scotland and he became the Detective Inspector for West Uist and Barra. He was thirty, well-built with raven black hair. His uncle, whom he had lived with ever since his parents had drowned in a boating accident in the Minch when he was a youngster, was sixty-six years old, but looked at least ten years younger with the healthy, weather-beaten complexion of an islander and a mane of white hair that defied the rule of brush and comb. With his horn-rimmed spectacles and clerical collar there was never a doubt about his calling.

'I can understand that, laddie,' Lachlan replied as he ladled out scrambled egg on a plate along with bacon, black pudding and tomatoes and laid it in front of his nephew. 'It's no fun for you and Lorna being apart so much of the time like this, especially when you've a wedding to plan for.'

Torquil started to butter a slice of toast while his uncle poured tea. 'Superintendent Lumsden is determined to make life difficult for us, just as he always has.'

Lachlan sat down and picked up his knife and fork in readiness to start on his breakfast. 'So he's not going to let her come back to the island permanently?'

Torquil gave a rueful laugh. 'Only on days off.'

Superintendent Lumsden had originally sent Sergeant Lorna Golspie to the island to do an efficiency study on the way Torquil ran the West Uist Police Station. He had expected her to report on a mountain of inefficiency, but instead they had solved a murder case together and fallen in love.

'He's moved house from Benbecula so that he can be on the spot at the headquarters. Now he sits like a spider in that office of his in Stornoway, weaving his web, working out ways of catching me in it,' Torquil said with a shrug.

Lachlan stirred his tea. 'He needs to learn how to forgive and then forget.'

'Easier said than done, Uncle. There has been bad blood between us ever since he was suspended from duty, pending investigation over that murder case I had been handling. I don't know what was said to him, but after he was reinstated, he's been even more of a stickler for the rulebook. He's an ambitious man with his eye on climbing to the top of the force. He can't really touch me now that I'm a DI, but if he can mess Lorna about and upset our plans then he'll do so.'

He told the Padre about the conversation he had just had with his fiancée about wedding favours.

'Ah, you have my sympathy there,' Lachlan replied. 'Wedding favours can always be tricky. Diplomacy and compromise, that's my advice. How about a bottle of cologne or aftershave instead of alcohol? Maybe some perfume for the ladies? Maisie McIvor on Harbour Street has a line in all these fragrances, if it is local you are wanting.'

Torquil pursed his lips. 'Aye, perhaps you are both right, although I know what some of the lads will think. But that's another dilemma I've got.'

The Padre sipped some tea and nodded his head. 'You mean that you haven't decided who you are going to have as your best man?'

Torquil blew air through his lips. 'Lorna had it easy. She's asked Morag's daughters to be her bridesmaids and Morag to be her matron of honour. My trouble is that I work with my friends and I see Calum Steele and Ralph McLelland almost every day. I wouldn't say any of them were exactly fawning over me, but in one way or another they all seem to be trying to curry favour.'

'An unenviable decision, my boy. Perhaps you should work out a handicap system to help you decide.'

His nephew almost choked on a mouthful of toast. 'I might have known you'd bring it down to golf, Uncle.'

The Padre chuckled. 'You may scoff, but the handicap is a perfect way of levelling things out according to ability. What other game allows a rank beginner to play against a professional and have a good chance of winning?'

'I don't see how it could help me.'

The Padre shrugged. 'Work out their best man handicaps. Just like making a balance sheet. Bad points, like being a garrulous creature likely to bring out your most humiliating experiences in his speech, would build the handicap up.'

'You're thinking of Calum, our esteemed editor of the *West Uist Chronicle*?'

'It would be wrong of me to name folk,' the Padre replied innocently. 'Good points, like being punctual, would reduce the handicap. You get my meaning?'

Torquil laughed. 'So are you golfing today?'

Lachlan McKinnon began clearing away the breakfast things. 'I think it is highly likely, once the mist clears enough to see the ball after a well struck drive with my three wood. How about yourself?'

Torquil took a last mouthful of tea and glanced at his watch. 'First, I'm going to the cave for a practice on the pipes to blow off a bit of steam, then I have to get down to the ferry to meet my new DC.'

'Of course, I had forgotten you have a newbie starting. It will increase your detective force by one hundred per cent, won't it?'

Torquil hummed. 'It will, which will be a help to me, as we will have responsibility for both West Uist, Barra, Eriskay and Benbecula. It'll be a challenge for her and no mistake.'

The Padre raised his eyebrows.

His nephew frowned. 'Now don't you jump on Lorna's bandwagon, Uncle. I merely meant it could challenge her because she's English. She's transferring straight here from Leeds. Do you think you could look after Crusoe?'

'With pleasure. I'll give him a run across the links to church. I think he likes the challenge of finding balls in the rough.'

Torquil gave a rueful smile. 'He's lucky that life is so uncomplicated. I would welcome a few less challenges in mine.'

CHAPTER TWO

PC Ewan McPhee had ridden 'Nippy,' his mother's old Morris 50 cc moped through the early Monday morning mist on his way up to the Hoolish Stones, passing by Dunshiffin Castle on the way. As he climbed higher the mist became fog and the moisture-laden atmosphere made myriads of spiderwebs stand out on the heather by the side of the gravel road whenever the headlight shone on them.

Every morning that he could, before going on duty and weather permitting, he liked to either go to the beach for a run along the sands and the machair, or head to the moor to practice his hammer throwing technique. The Western Isles champion at both wrestling and with the heavy hammer five times in a row, he worked hard to maintain his strength and his fitness. While he often moaned to his superior officers about not having official police transport, he secretly enjoyed riding the moped, especially since the machine was of the vintage where the pedals were actually functional, so he was able to give the machine a wee hand by using them on hills.

The vapours swirled, presenting variable visibility, sometimes closing in so that the moped's beam cut a mere fifteen feet or so into it, or it dissipated eerily to give reasonable views of the surrounding terrain. The road continued to rise gently through woodland and then opened out again into an undulating landscape of boulders and heather-covered moors with great swathes of bracken. Further over towards the coast there were a series of crofts with cottages both large and small, some of which had peat- or woodsmoke billowing from their chimneys, while others were unoccupied and some were falling into decay and dereliction. Others were such ancient ruins that no-one remembered who had once lived in them, or indeed, whether they had even been used for human habitation. Nettles and gorse swallowed them up or sheep and rabbits took up temporary residence.

During one of the more lucid breaks in the misty veil a glint of light from a nearby patch of bracken caught Ewan's eye and he realised that there was a figure crouched down. He automatically slowed down and stopped.

'*Madainn mhath*,' he called out. 'A good morning to you.'

Slowly, a figure rose from the heather. It was a man in a camouflage waterproof jacket and hat. In his hands he was holding a pair of binoculars. Ewan recognised Cameron Beamish, one half of the Kyleshiffin law practice. He was in his early forties, a stocky man of average height with a slightly round face. Large, round, black-framed spectacles rested on a small hooked nose and gave him a slightly owlish look.

'Hello there, Constable McPhee,' Cameron said, wading towards Ewan through the bracken. 'Are you on police business out on the moor at this hour?'

Ewan grinned and pointed to the pannier behind him from which protruded the stick of his hammer. 'No, just a spot of training. I'm headed further in where the ground is flat. I'll maybe frighten a few sheep or rabbits, I dare say. How about yourself?'

The solicitor raised his binoculars and laughed. 'Och, I'm just out doing a spot of birdwatching.'

'Birdwatching? I didn't know that was your thing.'

Cameron Beamish tapped the side of his nose. 'I keep it quiet, Ewan. I don't like folk to think of the local legal eagle as being a secret twitcher!'

Ewan gave a hearty laugh. 'I can see that might give the lads in the pub a laugh.'

'So, not a word, eh?'

Ewan patted Nippy's handlebars. 'Mum's the word, Cameron. I'd better get going if I want to get my practice in before work.' He grinned then added, jokingly: 'Happy twitching.'

Twenty minutes later Ewan was well into his practising.

'Oh, son of the devil!' he muttered to himself. 'Ewan McPhee, you have little chance of lifting a sixth title this year when you throw like an auld fish wife.' He strode over the heather to retrieve his hammer after his third throw.

Once again he wound himself up, whirling four times and then hurling for all he was worth. His curse came out of his mouth as soon as he turned to see the hammer sail through the air, forty-five degrees off target.

The Royal Mail van seemed to appear from nowhere. It came past a thicket of rowan trees and gorse bushes that had screened the road.

'No!' cried Ewan as the hammer began its descent and bounced on the road mere feet in front of the van.

Behind the wheel the driver slammed on the brake, causing the van to skid on the light gravel of the moor road and slew across it, coming to a halt inches in front of a ditch.

The driver opened the door as Ewan charged towards him through the heather.

'Were you actually trying to take out the Royal Mail, Constable McPhee, or did you just throw that hammer thingie of yours too far?'

Ewan jogged up to him, realising immediately that Stan Wilkinson, the relatively new rural postie, was joking. Ewan ran his fingers through his red hair and heaved a sigh of relief. 'I hadn't heard your van coming, Stan. The truth is that distance-wise it wasn't a half bad throw, but the direction was all to pot. I'm right sorry I made you stop.'

'No damage and no harm, Ewan,' Stan replied, dropping the official police title and grinning. He was a small wiry fellow with mousy brown hair and a full beard. Of a cheery disposition, he nodded at the hammer, which had bounced and rolled to the verge of the ditch, having left a small crater in the road surface. 'Well, no damage done, except you created a new pothole there.'

Ewan bit his lip. 'It's not exactly a pothole, Stan. More a dint, that's all.'

Stan winked. 'I was only kidding.'

'It wouldn't have happened if I had my proper shoes with me,' Ewan explained. He raised a foot and pointed to his sodden trainer. 'See this, it's useless. I cannot get any purchase with these things, so I've been trying to anchor myself in the heather. I broke one of the blades on my old murder shoes, you see.'

'Murder shoes?' Stan repeated, doubtfully. 'Did I hear you right, Ewan?'

Ewan suddenly laughed. 'Forgive me, Stan. I sometimes get too keen when talking about my sport. I assume folk know the lingo. When we throw the highland hammer we wear special footwear that we call murder shoes.'

'I'm still in the dark, Ewan. I've seen them tossing the hammer in athletics on the telly — not kicking them, so I don't see why you would need murder *shoes*?'

Ewan's eyes twinkled with merriment. 'Of course, you're English so you'll not have seen the proper hammer being thrown.' He picked up the hammer by the cane. 'The Olympic hammer thrower is allowed to rotate and spin like a discus thrower, but the highland hammer is thrown from a standing position. You need to be anchored, you see, so we wear boots or shoes with blades coming out the fronts. We dig them into the ground. They look like the shoes Olga Kleg wore in that James Bond story. Maybe you saw the film?'

Stan nodded enthusiastically. 'I know the one, *From Russia With Love*. I can just see her clicking her heels together and a knife blade shoots out, dipped in poison, I think?' He chuckled.

'Aye, calling them murder shoes is just a wee joke in the hammer-throwing fraternity, you see. Talking of them, I'm due some new ones any day in the post. Could you have a rummage in that van for me? They'll be addressed to the station.'

Stan thrust his hands deep into his pockets and shoved himself away from the van. He shook his head apologetically. 'I can't help, Ewan. It would be more than my job's worth to do that. I'm not supposed to give mail before I arrive at the address. Rules, you see.'

Ewan nodded emphatically. 'Of course, I shouldn't have put you in such an awkward position, Stan. I apologise.'

Stan climbed into his seat and pulled the door closed. 'No problem, Constable McPhee. Just be patient, and if your murder shoes are here, I'll be delivering them later on when I get back to Kyleshiffin.'

Ewan laughed and then watched the Royal Mail van drive off, soon disappearing in the mist. *That Stan is a good fellow*, he thought. *That's just what we need on West Uist, chaps like him with a natural respect for rules and the law. And gentle types like Cameron Beamish too, who care about nature.*

He chuckled to himself as he thought of the owlish solicitor with his high-powered binoculars. *Aye, in this mist he'll need all the help he can get to spot any birds at all.*

The Kyleshiffin police station was a converted pebble-dashed bungalow off Lady's Wynd, which ran parallel to Harbour Street. After his training session Ewan McPhee had let himself in and then locked the door and changed into his regulation Police Scotland uniform, which they were now forced to wear instead of the casual blue Arran sweaters that they used pre-2013 when they were just members of the Hebridean Constabulary. Now they had to wear black trousers, matching black wicking top with zip-up collar, epaulettes with numbers and rank and a utility belt with all the accoutrements of law enforcement. Ewan didn't mind it at all, but he was aware that the others resented it, especially when they had to wear high-vis jackets and caps.

At quarter to eight he nipped out to Allardyce, the baker's shop on Harbour Street to get a supply of butter rolls for when the others arrived. He planned to make the tea when he returned, so it was fresh for them.

There was a queue inside the shop already.

'*Latha math*. And it's a good morning to the big lawman himself,' said a small tubby man in a yellow anorak, wearing thick spectacles. Ahead of him a young woman turned and smiled at Ewan.

'Hello Ewan, what time do you call this?' she asked, with an impish grin.

'Good morning Calum and Cora. Don't tell me, the *West Uist Chronicle*'s news team have been up all night working on the next issue,' Ewan replied, cheerily.

'Aye, you got it in one, Ewan,' said Calum. He leaned towards the big policeman and spoke in hushed tones lest any of the other customers should hear. 'The truth is, we were scratching our heads about what to put in. There's been nothing happening lately and we've been scouring the internet to write feature articles. We've written a long one about you, actually.'

'He's only kidding,' said Cora, elbowing the editor of the local newspaper in the ribs. 'We've been plenty busy. We at the *West Uist Chronicle* are now 24/7 purveyors of the news with our newspaper, website, blog and Facebook page.'

'You mean you are dragging Calum screaming into the digital age, Cora?'

Cora Melville giggled and slipped her arms around her boss — and boyfriend's —waist and gave him a kiss on the cheek. 'He needs a bit of dragging around sometimes,' she added with another giggle.

Gordon Allardyce, a ruddy-faced, middle-aged bachelor and notorious flirt winked at Cora as he reached behind the counter for some pies for the customer he was serving. 'You could drag me around anytime, sweetheart. Besides, you never know which gutter the editor of our local rag has been wallowing in.'

Calum knocked a knuckle on the glass counter. 'We'll have less of the flirting with my chief reporter if you don't mind, Gordon. And a bit more respect for the press. After all, we have the law beside us today and if you're not careful we'll tell him what you lace your pasties with.'

A few minutes later the two journalists and Ewan emerged onto the mist-shrouded Harbour Street which was beginning to get busy at the start of the day.

'Look, there's Nathan Westwood and Helen Beamish over by the harbour wall,' said Calum as he took a bite on a mutton pie. 'Let's have a chat. I like to watch an artist at work.' He nodded towards the harbour where a tall man in a rollneck sweater and chinos was leaning against the wall sketching something on an artist's pad, while chatting to a petite, striking woman with auburn hair tied back in a ponytail.

Ewan glanced at his watch. 'I'm afraid I've got to open the station up, so I'd better be on my way.' Clutching his bag of butter rolls he touched his cap in a half salute and strode off towards Lady's Wynd.

'*Latha math* — good morning to you both,' Calum said, announcing his approach halfway across the road. 'What on earth are you drawing in this mizzle, Nathan? Are you not getting your paper wet?'

Nathan Westwood was an Englishman who ran Westwood's Art and Antique Gallery, a pink-facaded shop with two large bay windows halfway along Harbour Street. In one half of the gallery he displayed his own watercolour paintings and those of other Western Isles artists, while in the other half he ran a thriving antique business.

Nathan turned round and laid his sketch pad on the wall beside a bridge camera. 'Good morning to you all,' he greeted in a smooth Surrey accent. 'Wonderful foggy day, isn't it?'

Cora wrinkled her nose. 'I wouldn't call it wonderful, exactly. It's a bit *dreich*.'

Helen Beamish laughed. 'That's exactly what I was explaining to him. It's cheerless, dismal and to be expected in Scotland.'

Nathan shook his head with a broad smile. 'But I don't see it in those terms. Look at it, it's wonderful stuff. It swirls, it scintillates and it makes everything so magical and mysterious. Look at the masts of the boats down there. Ghostly shapes, aren't they? And the sight of the ferries coming in when it's like this is a sight to behold. That's why I photograph it and make sketches whenever it seems right to catch it. Mist, mizzle and fog, I love the way they all blur and soften what you see.'

'Catching mist must be like capturing moonbeams,' said Calum with a chuckle. He turned and pointed at Nathan's gallery with his pie. 'Yet you obviously do all right by painting it, judging by the Jaguar you have parked outside your gallery.'

Helen Beamish gave Calum a friendly tap on the arm. 'Calum Steele, you shouldn't say things like that. It's not polite.'

'I think what Calum meant to say was that he likes your car,' Cora said to Nathan with one of the sweet apologetic smiles that she had learned to use when Calum had been bullish, over-zealous or just downright rude to someone.

The artist smiled. 'I understand. I am fortunate to have people who like my work enough to keep buying it. And my antiques. The internet helps, of course.'

'Exactly what I keep telling Calum,' said Cora. 'You have to have a digital presence.'

'Everyone does these days,' Helen agreed. 'It's a must in law practice.' She looked at her watch. 'Talking of which, I'll need to go, too. I'll catch you later about that watercolour commission for my office, Nathan.'

As Helen went, Nathan picked up his camera and sketchpad and smiled at the *West Uist Chronicle* duo. 'Why don't you drop into the gallery sometimes, Cora. I can show you some of my misty pictures and convince you that there is magic in dreich, as you called it.' He nodded goodbye and sauntered across the street to leave the editor and his assistant to contemplate the mist over the harbour.

'So what now, boss? I'm not ready to sleep yet. Shall we wander about looking for news or wait for an ambulance to chase?'

Calum laughed. 'What did I tell you the other day about tempting providence. It's a good thing we're not superstitious. Let's wait for the ferry to come in out of the mist and see if we can see the magic that Nathan says is around it.'

'Why not take a few pictures?' Cora snapped her fingers. 'We could maybe start a regular slot in the *Chronicle* of pictures of the island in the mist. I'm thinking of a catchy title, like Dreich Sketches, or Magical Mist-ery Tours. You know, a play on the Beatles.'

Calum laughed and gave her a peck on the cheek. 'You're getting the hang of this, my wee darling. Also, you never know, there might just be someone interesting coming over on the ferry.'

After washing and putting the breakfast things away and then dealing with a couple of parish matters over the phone the Padre picked up his golf bag and let himself out of the back door of the manse. He went down the drive, crossed the road and mounted the old stile that led onto the ten-acre plot of undulating dunes and machair that he and several other local worthies had years before transformed into the St Ninian's Golf Course.

Using the natural lie of the land they had constructed six holes with billiard smooth greens surrounded by barbed wire square fences to keep the sheep off, in contrast to the coarse grass fairways where they were allowed to graze freely. Each hole had three separate tee positions, each one giving its route to the hole a special name in both English and Gaelic, thereby allowing players the choice of following the conventional eighteen holes or any combination. The Padre was proud of telling people that while it was not exactly St Andrews, it was a good test of golf.

It was his habit to play three random holes on his way to St Ninian's church and he was relieved that the fog had lifted enough to make golf possible, at least for a while. He stood for a few moments by the honesty box, where players could deposit their green fee and stuffed tobacco from his old yellow oilskin pouch into an equally old cracked briar pipe. Then, lighting it, he picked up his bag and strode over the hillock to the first hole.

A man was standing on the tee, about to drive off.

'Ah, Padre, you are just in time to join me, if you have a mind for some company?'

'George, *latha math*. This is a surprise, but it would be a pleasure. I'm just playing three holes on my way to the kirk. You are out early. Does that distillery of yours not need you any longer?'

George Corlin-MacLeod, the co-owner with his wife of the Glen Corlin estate and its famous whisky distillery, grinned, showing perfect, Hollywood-white teeth, quite in keeping with the local celebrity image that he enjoyed and cultivated. He was a handsome fifty-something, who looked far younger, thanks to the wonders of cosmetic surgery, which both he and his wife, Esther Corlin-MacLeod could afford to indulge in.

'Lachlan, you know very well that the distillery has little need of me, at least not for the whisky production. Esther does far more of the running than I do. I'm more use in advertising, promotion and overseas sales.'

'Have you brought a sample in a hipflask then?' the Padre asked with a grin.

George shook his head and smiled apologetically. 'I'm afraid not, Lachlan. Although I promote our products, I don't imbibe very often. Esther's parents and her late cousin, from whom we inherited the business, put me off drinking.'

The Padre nodded sagely. 'I understand, George. I was only teasing.'

'I'm already teed up, so are you all right with ready golf?'

The Padre nodded. 'Away you go.'

George took a couple of practice swings before launching himself into his drive. There was a resounding click and the ball shot away on a slight left to right trajectory to land two hundred and eighty yards or so in the light rough on the right, just within the limits of visibility in the mist.

'Good drive, George,' said the Padre, pulling his three wood from his old canvas golf pencil bag.

'Still using the wooden headed clubs, Lachlan? You must be one of the last golfers to do so.'

'Aye, I cannot abide that hollow, tin can sound these modern affairs make. I'm an unashamed traditionalist, you see.' He teed his ball up, took a single practice swing and then drove the ball with his usual controlled draw two hundred and sixty yards into the middle of the fairway.

'Bravo, Lachlan. Effortless efficiency.'

They walked down the fairway together until they came to Lachlan's ball. He gauged the remaining distance and with an easy swing lobbed the ball onto the green to roll up to ten feet from the hole. A few moments later George took out a pitching wedge and matched the Padre's shot. On the green they each two putted and halved the hole in pars.

Lachlan patted George on the shoulder. 'That's good enough, for a gimme. Now would you like to tell me why you really came out to the course today? I know when I've been ambushed.'

George Corlin-MacLeod grimaced. 'Actually, you are right, I have a problem that I'd like your advice on. The thing is — it's really a wee bit difficult. Awkward, even!'

Lachlan pointed to the whitewashed church. 'Why don't we adjourn to my place of work, then, George? The pews will all be empty this morning and my boss up above likes to test me with things difficult and awkward.'

For the second time that morning Stan Wilkinson was shocked to look out the side window of his van and see someone charging at him. This time it was a woman, waving her arms like windmills as she ran through the heather covered slopes from the pillbox on Harpoon Hill. He recognised her as Morag Driscoll, the local police sergeant.

He stopped and pressed the button to lower the window. 'Sergeant Driscoll, what can I —?' he began.

'Ah, Stan Wilkinson, if ever I needed someone, it's certainly yourself. I have an emergency on my hands and I have no phone.'

The postman climbed quickly out of his van and pulled his phone from his pocket. He unlocked it and handed it to her and listened in awe as she briefly explained the situation while she coded in Doctor Ralph McLelland's number.

'Teenagers. Three of them have been drinking all night up in the old pillbox. One's dead, I'm sorry to say, and one's got visual trouble and can't see.'

'Christ Almighty!' Stan exclaimed, his jaw dropping and his face paling instantly. 'I saw Constable McPhee earlier on my round. Should I drive back and see if I can find him. Maybe he—'

Morag raised a hand to silence him while she spoke to Ralph McLelland. Then once she had finished: 'There is no point. Ewan McPhee will have been practising his hammer throwing, I am thinking. He's probably back at the police station by now. I'm going to need you to take Catriona McDonald up to Kyleshiffin Cottage Hospital. Doctor McLelland said he'll meet you in the accident and emergency room.'

She next called the station and was relieved when Ewan answered immediately. She dispensed with niceties and quickly issued instructions to him before turning to Stan. 'Right, now let's get Catriona,' she ordered in her no-nonsense professional manner, as she led the way up the slope.

A few moments later Catriona McDonald, no longer sobbing or screaming, but clearly in shock, was strapped into the passenger seat of the Royal Mail van. Morag told her to stop rubbing her eyes and to just keep them closed with her hands over them, to rest them until the doctor saw her.

'You said there were three, so what about the third one?' Stan asked, circling the van to get into the driver's seat.

'That's just what I need to find out. I had a look to make sure she hadn't fallen over the cliff in this fog and thank god she hasn't. I'll get our special constables, the Drummond lads, up here to help.' As Stan held his hand out for his phone she shrugged her shoulders apologetically. 'I'm afraid that as it's such an emergency I'm going to have to ask you to leave your phone with me.'

Stan hesitated for a moment, then nodded with a thin smile. 'Of course. You'll need my pass code number. It's 1066.'

'Ah, the Battle of Hastings,' Morag mused. 'I can remember that fine. I'll get it back to you once I get back to the station and charge my own up. Now, please Stan, be quick, but drive safely.'

As she made her way back up over the heather slope Morag realised that she was now shaking. Jamie Mackintosh was only a few years older than her girls and now he was dead. They'd been drinking themselves stupid all night and all of them were underage. Celebrating finishing exams, she guessed.

Damn! Damn! Damn! Why the hell couldn't I do anything for Jamie? The important question now is where on earth is Vicky Spiers?

She felt sick, but suppressed the urge to vomit as she had no time even for that. Before she went back into the pillbox to begin doing the things she needed to do, she called Torquil's number. There was no answer and it went straight onto voicemail. She left a message to call her urgently. A minute later she called again, with the same result.

Then she felt unable to hold back the wave of nausea any longer. She ran back down the slope to the roadside and vomited some distance from the pillbox. She had been careful not to contaminate a potential crime scene.

The killer was not prone to self-doubt. Yet there were differences between the mundane considerations of normal life and the inevitably pedantic ruminations that followed a murder.

Have I left any sort of clue? Is there anything that could link me to the bastard? Was I too sure of myself and made a stupid mistake that the local plods might fathom out?

Such thoughts had been nagging away every minute of every hour since the killing. All the bits and pieces that needed to be disposed of had either been destroyed or washed and discreetly discarded. The laptop had been thoroughly searched and any suspicious files had been carefully disposed of. There was no link.

My god! But there is something I haven't thought of.

I'll have to risk it and go back.

But, no. It's a thousand to one that anyone will notice. I'll leave it and trust in fate.

CHAPTER THREE

Torquil had taken the snaking headland road on his classic Royal Enfield Bullet 500. Visibility in the mist was not too bad, allowing him to open up the throttle and zoom past Loch Hynish with its crannog and ancient ruin, passing along the edge of the machair, the sand on peat meadow that intervened between the heather covered Corlin Hills and the seaweed strewn beaches below.

A couple of miles on he took the fork down towards the deserted fishermen's hamlet of Cabhail and parked in the isolated layby, then jumped down and scrunched across the shingle beech to the entrance of St Ninian's Cave, one of his favourite places in the world.

The great basalt columned cave had been used by generations of island pipers, including his uncle, the Padre. He remembered the day when he had first taken him and his pipes and introduced him to the cave's special magic. The young Torquil had hoped that he would one day follow in his uncle's footsteps and become a champion piper and winner of the Silver Quaich. Much to their mutual pleasure he duly did, so that there now resided a Silver Quaich on each end of the mantelpiece in the manse's sitting room.

Nature had carved this sea cave beautifully, so that it seemed to hold a sound perfectly for a moment and Torquil was able to hear the correct pitch of his playing. It was a natural tape recorder for a musician.

For a couple of minutes he ran through his repertoire of warm-up exercises, to get his finger movements right. He played a string of leumluaths, taorluaths, grace notes and birls.

Then he played a couple of reels, a strathspey and a piobaireachd. He found it an excellent start to the day and a great way of problem-solving, because strangely enough the pipe music always cleared his head and allowed him to see solutions.

He felt the need of such help this morning after his conversation with Lorna over the wedding favours, as well as his dilemma about who would be his best man.

He felt altogether in much higher spirits when he emerged from the cave to return to the Bullet, albeit no clearer about his choice of best man. Stowing his pipes in the panier he saw that he had left his mobile phone in the other one. Picking it up he found nine missed calls and nine voicemails, all from a phone number he did not recognise.

'Damnation,' he muttered angrily at himself. 'I'm an idiot all right, leaving my phone here. Someone wants me urgently.'

He called his voicemail and was surprised to hear Morag's voice. All of the messages were from her and each successive one was a curt rejoinder to call her immediately on this number, until the last one, spoken in an icy tone: 'DI McKinnon, it's me again! I need to speak to you urgently as this is a matter for both uniform and detective branch. Wallace and Douglas Drummond, our special constables are with me now. We have an extreme emergency situation at the pillbox on Harpoon Hill. We have taped off the area and I am sending them out to search for a missing teenager. I am at the scene waiting for you to attend. Call me as soon as you receive this and I'll give you the details. I repeat — this is extremely urgent!'

He did as she bid and listened in horror and disbelief as she briefly recounted the events of the morning.

Putting on his Cromwell helmet and adjusting his Mark Nine goggles he started up the Bullet and, doing a U-turn, accelerated into the mist.

The local office of Comhairle nan Eilean Siar, the Western Isles Council was on the first floor of the Duncan Institute, a strawberry-pink-faced building right in the middle of Harbour Street. All of the buildings and shop fronts on the crescent shaped street were different colours and all of them were maintained through a council grant, justified because it helped the local tourist industry.

The Western Isles council, administering the Outer Hebrides and whose main office was in Stornoway in the Isle of Lewis was the only council in the whole of Scotland to have retained the official name in Gaelic. It was a decision that Councillor Charlie McDonald completely agreed with. A staunch Scottish Nationalist Party member for his entire political life he had a vision of a Scotland independent from the United Kingdom, which would need, in his view, a part of it to retain its roots and its ancient language. That part, he believed should be the Hebrides and some of the West coast of Scotland, for this had been the region where the Gaelic had been spoken for centuries. He had lobbied hard to have all road signs labelled in the two languages of English and Gaelic.

All of this was the nationalist view that he promulgated to the people of his ward and which everyone believed. The truth known only to himself was a different matter. Charlie McDonald was an opportunist. Although he had made his name in local politics, he had loftier ambitions, and had set his sights upon one day becoming the Member of the Scottish Parliament, or MSP, for the Na h'Eileanan an Iar — the constituency of the Scottish Parliament — which had exactly the same boundaries as the Western Isles Council. The present MSP was in rude good health, though, so he knew that he would have to just bide his time, stay in the public eye and remain popular.

Charlie McDonald knew only too well that maintaining popularity as a politician was not an easy matter, if one wished to stick strictly to the book. Being a pragmatist, he was prepared to curry favours and use whatever means were needed to gain advantages to those constituents that mattered most to him, while still doing the job for the better good of the many. It was important, of course, never to be seen to be biased.

He was a forty-two-year-old bachelor who owned a fishing business and also ran a croft with his brother on the south of the island, having worked both with his father until his sudden death a couple of years previously. His complexion was ruddy from his outdoor life, albeit not weather-beaten as were so many of his age. When working on his boat or on his croft he wore the appropriate working clothes, but when doing council work, as he was this day, he dressed in a jacket, collar and tie.

Sitting behind his pine desk piled with paperwork from his work on the Sustainable Development committee, which oversaw and looked after matters to do with crofting, fishing, conservation and tourism, he was feeling more fraught than usual as he conducted his weekly morning surgery, when local residents and constituents either arrived for an appointment or dropped in on spec. Starting at his regular hour of seven o'clock he had seen and dealt with a dozen requests, enquiries and grievances by quarter past nine. As usual he had made copious notes of things that he would attend to later, whether by phone, letter or email. He prided himself on never being absent or late for surgery. Seven was a good time to start, he felt, even in the long dark days of winter, since no one could say he was not there for them.

His last client had really tested his patience and it had taken all of his political skills and considerable wiles to deflect the questions and his aggressive manner. There had been much finger-jabbing, desk thumping and more than a little cursing in both Gaelic and English. The case was more complicated than most, for it crossed the boundary between councillor and constituent and veered into the murky waters of personal business.

. He was running his hands through his hair with his elbows on his desk when Archie Reid, his secretary, knocked and immediately came in. Archie was a wiry fellow in his early sixties with pebble-thick spectacles, wearing a cardigan over a grey shirt and a neatly pressed tie. He was known locally as Archie Many Hats, on account of the fact that he had several jobs and managed to inveigle himself into various odd job positions, such as the five hours a week he was paid by the council to look after Charlie McDonald's surgery and sort his mail. Apart from that he had two businesses at the far end of Harbour Street. The first was a tobacconist and sweet shop and next door to it he had run a smokehouse. Archie Reid's Smoked Kippers were highly popular on West Uist and on Barra, Eriskay and Benbecula.

Never one to stand on ceremony, Archie said, 'It's as well that I'm near as deaf as a post despite these hearing aids that Doctor McLelland arranged or I fear I'd be reporting the bad language coming out of this office. Yon Hamish McNab was fair shouting and cursing.'

Charlie McDonald nodded with a smile. He actually suspected that Archie heard well enough even without his hearing aids and he was not entirely sure that his vision was half as bad as merited his thick lensed spectacles. 'Sorry about that, Archie, but you know that it was him doing all the swearing, not me. Was there anyone out there in the waiting room?'

'Luckily not. He strutted out of here in a fair temper, though.'

'That's because he was cross.'

'Aye, I gathered that. What was he wanting —?'

'I cannot say, Archie, you know that.'

'It'll either have been about his distillery or the crofting, then,' replied Archie. 'By the way, your old wife rang.'

Charlie frowned. 'You mean my *ex*-wife, Bridget. Although I'm not her biggest fan anymore, she's only forty-two, and that doesn't make her old, Archie. She's still only about half your age.'

Archie eyed him distastefully. *'Contrachd ort!* Curse you! Anyway, she sounded in a fair dither and wants you to call her back straight away.' He jabbed a finger in the direction of the phone. 'Urgent, she said. If I were you I'd make her your first call.'

'Any mail?'

'Not yet. It's not like that new postie to be late, so maybe no one wants to write to you anymore.'

Charlie called his ex-wife Bridget, expecting that she wanted to harangue him about money.

'Why didn't you call me right away,' she asked shrilly.

He sighed. It hadn't always been like that between them. He had loved her once, even hung on her every word instead of cringing at the sound of her voice as he did now. He had to admit that he was no innocent, he had wronged her by having an affair. A stupid liaison that meant nothing to him, but unfortunately had meant everything to that stupid cow, Peggy,

Bridget's one-time best friend. She had thought that the best way to win him forever was to tell Bridget that they were having an affair and wanted to be together. Bridget was always one to fire from the hip. She went bananas and divorced him, and he duly ditched Peggy. He should have felt guilty, but he didn't. He enjoyed being a relatively free agent.

The thing was he was only free half the time. He was still Catriona's father and she was the apple of his eye. Acrimonious though the divorce had been both he and Bridget agreed to share custody and to bring her up and give her the best opportunities they could.

'She's not been home all night,' Bridget stated sharply.

There was a moment's silence which both he and Bridget expected to fill.

'Well, where has she been?' he asked. 'She's with you Sunday to Wednesday, and this is Monday.'

'She said she was staying with you and that you said it was OK. She was going on from Vicky's house.'

'Vicky Spiers?'

'Of course! What other Vicky does she know?'

Sarcasm, always sarcasm, he thought.

'You're hopeless, Charlie McDonald! So where is she? Did she even go to her job this morning? She's only sixteen, for God's sake.'

'You don't know if she's gone to work?'

'There's no reply at the Hydro, it just went straight to their call-back message.'

Charlie sighed. He could see that she was in one of her 'it's your fault' moods. 'They'll be busy, that's all, Bridgie.'

'Don't call me that!' she snapped. 'Find out now.'

The phone went dead in his hand and he replaced it on the receiver. Almost immediately Archie tapped once on the door and came straight in.

'While you were on the phone Mrs Esther Corlin-MacLeod rang me in reception wanting you to call her. She says you know her number. And just a minute later Mrs Helen Beamish the solicitor did the same as well.' He stood on the other side of the desk with his hands deep in his pockets. 'Was that about Catriona?'

Charlie frowned and declined to answer. 'Not so much wrong with the hearing aids today, is there, Archie? Now, away and make some tea while I make a few calls.'

Archie gave him one of his sour looks. 'You should have taken better care of your old wife. Bridget was a treasure, you ken.'

Charlie pulled one of his practiced smiles. 'Tea, Archie?'

When Archie left he picked up the phone and smiled, debating with himself which call to make first. He was much in demand it seemed. He wondered what either of the women in question wanted. His lips curled into a leer as he imagined the two of them lying naked in the heather and him standing over them with a choice to make.

He dialled the number that immediately came into his head.

Torquil raced back along the road for a mile and then went off-road to weave his way along old rutted tracks through the gorse to reach the old road leading up to Harpoon Hill.

Morag was waiting outside, still just in her jogging kit, running on the spot with her arms crossed so she could rub her upper arms to keep warm. Behind her police barrier tape had been strung on canes around the pillbox and across the entrance.

'You must be frozen, Morag,' he called up as he pulled the Bullet onto its stand and took off his helmet. He ran up the slope, peeling off his leather jacket on the way so that he could drape it round her shoulders. 'I'm sorry I left my phone while I was practising at St Ninian's cave.' He shook his head in disbelief. 'This is a tragedy and no mistake.'

His sergeant's pained expression and pale face told him how much of an ordeal she had found the situation. 'I got Ewan to send up the barrier tape with the twins. We've strung it six feet clear all the way about the pillbox just in case. I sent them off to look for Vicky Spiers.'

He patted her shoulder. 'Good work. So, Jamie's inside?'

Tears had formed in her eyes and she nodded. 'I couldn't do anything for him, Torquil.'

'I'm sure you did what you could, Morag. And Ralph McLelland is going to see Catriona McDonald?'

'Aye, it's fortunate that Stan Wilkinson was on his round and was coming along when he did. She can't see anything, Torquil. The poor kid's hysterical.'

He nodded. 'Right, let's take a look.'

'Brace yourself, Piper,' she said, using the nickname Torquil's friends on the island often called him.

They ducked under the tape and entered the dark interior of the pillbox.

'They put cardboard boxes over the windows and I left them in case the forensics need to see everything as it was. There's a lantern just inside, which I switched off when I ... when I stopped my resuscitation attempt. I ... I thought they might be able to work out how long it had been on from its charge.'

'You just stay here at the entrance then,' Torquil told her, conscious that her voice was quaking.

The pillbox was a hexagonal structure built of reinforced concrete, with a Y-shaped wall inside that was not complete, so that men would have been able to walk round it from one embrasure to the next. It was designed thus to limit ricocheting bullets should it be targeted and it effectively divided it into two spaces and an entrance area. As Morag had said, it was dark because of the cardboard boxes the teenagers had blocked up the embrasures with. In the right hand one he saw the body of Jamie Mackintosh.

'I tried CPR for twenty minutes, Torquil,' Morag said from behind him. 'That's why the blanket is thrown aside there. And I took another one and wrapped it round Catriona.'

'Did you take photographs?'

'Aye, but this isn't my phone so I'll send them to my own phone and get them when I charge it up. Then I'd better delete them from Stan's phone.'

'Better not just yet,' Torquil said over his shoulder. 'Just in case they don't get through to yours. We'd best impound Stan's phone until we've sorted everything out with the Procurator Fiscal.'

Kneeling down, Torquil cursorily inspected the body, careful not to disturb anything else. Reaching for his own phone he took several pictures and then stood up to look round the pillbox.

'He had been frothing at the mouth,' Morg explained. 'It looked like he'd had a fit, or some sort of seizure. Maybe he'd inhaled vomit. Anyway, I cleared his mouth before I gave him CPR. When I began chest compressions some dirty vomit came out of his mouth.'

Torquil nodded and looked around the pillbox. 'So there are two blankets here, one belonging to Jamie beside his body, and one by the wall.'

'That will be Vicky Spiers's.'

'Oatcakes, empty crisp bags, three cans of Coke and an empty bottle of whisky,' he said out loud as he photographed them and their positions. 'It does no harm to have more pictures.' He stood up and looked round to see Morag standing at the entrance, studiously avoiding looking at the teenager's body. 'There's no label on the bottle,' he noted.

'Catriona reeked of whisky and so did Jamie,' Morag returned. Her hand went unconsciously to wipe her mouth. 'I gave him mouth to mouth. The fumes almost knocked me out.'

Torquil knelt down and sniffed the empty bottle. '*Daingead!* I see what you mean. It's peatreek, and bloody strong at that. I'm betting they were washing it down with Coke.' Straightening up, he nodded at his sergeant. 'Let's get outside. We'll need to get a Scene Examiner over from Lewis.'

Up until 2013, when the West Uist was part of the Hebridean Constabulary, they would have handled this entirely inhouse. Morag had undergone CID training in Dundee as a young officer, thereby picking up forensic experience before returning to West Uist, marriage and parenthood. She and Doctor Ralph McLelland, the local GP and police surgeon, who was also a qualified pathologist, had worked as an unofficial forensic team. With the amalgamation of all eight of the Scottish regional police forces into the national Police Scotland, everything had changed, and regulations were strictly enforced. Now they had to bring in a Scene Examiner, a specially trained civilian employed by the Scottish Police Authority to collect evidence, which would then be passed to Torquil as the local DI and to the forensic lab on the mainland.

It was with this all in mind that Morag and Torquil had taken so many photographs and taken good care not to disturb the scene of the sudden death of the teenager.

Outside, the mist had turned into mizzle as the fog descended, and therefore visibility had started to recede to fifty yards, as it was liable to do in the Western Isles. Looking up at the sky with a frown, Morag called the station and issued further instructions to Ewan McPhee.

'Tell him to say that we urgently need this whisky bottle analysing,' Torquil said over his shoulder. 'Say we're pretty sure it's peatreek, but we suspect it's got a high level of methyl alcohol in it.'

Morag transmitted the message. Then: 'That's exactly what I thought, boss. What with Catriona losing her sight and poor Jamie Mackintosh dying suddenly.'

Although technically Torquil was no longer her boss, since she was now uniform and he detective branch, they had continued to work together in the way they were used to, for it worked so well. She just made sure she stayed on the right side of Superintendent Lumsden.

Torquil nodded. 'We really need Ralph McLelland up here to certify death before we can notify his parents. We've got to get moving on this.'

'He's going to have his hands full dealing with Catriona. That's if he can do anything to help her,' Morag added.

'Aye, and there is Vicky Spiers to find. Let's hope the weather lifts, because it isn't helping. There simply aren't enough of us, Morag.' He glanced at his watch and took a rapid intake of breath. 'Nèamhan math! Good heavens, the new Detective Constable. I'm supposed to be meeting her off the ferry.'

CHAPTER FOUR

The Old Hydro Residential Home stood on a rise above Kyleshiffin, reached by taking the first right on Lady Wynd and following a zigzag road up the hill. It had been a hydropathic hotel back in Edwardian times before the Great War, when hydrotherapy and the water cure were all the rage. Nowadays, like so many such establishments it had been transformed into a residential home catering for the senior citizens for West Uist.

Norma Ferguson was the assistant manager, a position she was extremely proud to have reached at the age of twenty-three. A homely young woman, she loved her job caring for the older folk, many of whom she had known all of her life. She felt part of living history watching them be admitted, nurturing their ailments and listening to whatever baggage they brought with them.

The trouble was she had to work such long and arduous hours, because getting staff and retaining them was never easy. The fact that several of the residents had mild cognitive impairment, or even Alzheimer's disease or one of the other types of dementia, made it exhausting, because one had to be continually vigilant to keep them safe.

Breakfast was a demanding time and Norma was always relieved when the part-time girls called in to help her. There were currently three of them, all pupils at Kyleshiffin Community Academy studying for their Highers. Unfortunately, she knew that soon there was a good chance that they would all be off to university and then they'd have to start recruiting all over again.

'Where's the man himself?' asked Doreen McGuire, one of the older care assistants, referring to Norma's manager, Robbie Ochterlonie. 'I know he's had his two days off, but he's always put in a show by now when he's back on duty. I'm struggling a bit with breakfasts as it is. I hope his diabetes isn't playing up.'

Norma shrugged. 'He's not been in touch with me.' She glanced at the grandfather clock, its face being an old advert for a homeopathic chemist based in Oban. Doreen was right, Robbie was always on time. And she knew that they were also two care assistants down. Neither Catriona McDonald nor Vicky Spiers had shown up or even called in.

Millie McKendrick, another of the older care assistants, sidled past with a large teapot in each hand. She snorted derisively and whispered from the side of her mouth: 'Or maybes he's had a bit too much of that peatreek of his. You know, the stuff he peddles to old Stuart and his pals.' She nodded in the direction of a table of four occupied by three elderly men and a refined looking lady with snow white hair.

Norma scowled at the older care assistant. 'That's enough of that, Millie. We don't want any gossip of that sort.'

'Please yourself,' retorted Millie. 'It's just another possibility to think of. The boss knows what I think of strong liquor, for I've told him often enough.'

Norma felt a strange shiver run up and down her spine as she picked up a tray with four helpings of bacon and eggs.

'I'll need to check up on them all once we've got the breakfasts done and everyone sorted,' she said pensively. 'Maybe there's just a bug or something going round.'

In his role as Cora's mentor, Calum always emphasised that a good local journalist had to regard every conversation as a potential lead to a story. Which was why after leaving Nathan

Westwood they had ambled up Harbour Street, engaging the various business and shop owners in conversation wherever the opportunity arose. However, Calum was not insightful enough to realise that sometimes a quick reversal of direction by folk upon seeing him could be due to avoidance behaviour.

Tam MacOnachie, the harbour master and proprietor of MacOnachie Chandlery, had no such opportunity to beat a retreat as the mist was particularly thick at the top of Harbour Street, and they approached him under its cover, appearing only when they were twenty yards distant from him.

MacOnachie Chandlery was an establishment that sold everything pertaining to fishing and sailing, as well as having a good supply of groceries. At the back was Tam's workshop where he performed repairs on all manner of gear relating to the sea. He himself was a man of about seventy with weather-beaten skin and a ring of hair around his head that gave the bald dome above it the look of a boiled egg. Indeed, it was for that reason that some years before the Drummond twins had nicknamed him 'Eggy' MacOnachie, much to his annoyance and their glee. The name had stuck locally and everyone knew him as such when they were out of his hearing.

Tam was putting out a rack of assorted beach toys, junior fishing rods and crabbing nets in front of the chandlery. As usual he was wearing his brown shop-coat with an oiled apron on top and with his trousers tucked into his aged Wellington boots. About his neck hung a pair of binoculars.

'Not much to see today, Tam,' said Calum. 'Not with all this mist.'

'It'll clear in an hour or so,' replied Tam, phlegmatically. 'The ferry will have come and gone by then. Let's hope there are plenty of holiday makers coming.'

'It's a pretty dismal welcome to them though,' Cora chipped in. 'All this mist and fog.'

'Aye well, it may be dreich, but at least it's not chucking down.'

Cora laughed. 'We were talking to Nathan Westwood earlier and he was sketching the mist. He was telling us that he finds it mysterious, not dreich.'

Tam snorted. 'Anything that reduces visibility near water is just a hazard in my view, so I'm no fan of it. But it's nature and we canna change it so we have to just live with it. As for mysteries, I prefer mine in paperbacks.'

They chatted for a few moments until with a glance at his watch, Tam removed his apron and went inside to deposit it on the counter. A moment later he returned wearing his white peaked harbourmaster's hat and carrying a battered leather briefcase. 'Right then, as I said, it'll soon be time for the ferry so I'd better get down to do my duties.'

Suddenly, from the other end of the street came the sound of a vehicle. A red Royal Mail van came out of the mist with its headlights on full, its hazard warning lights flashing and its horn peeping.

'*Creideamh!*' exclaimed Calum. 'That's Stan Wilkinson, moving a bit fast for these conditions. It's lucky for him Ewan McPhee isn't here.'

The van came along Harbour Street towards them, its windscreen wipers moving furiously back and forth.

'There's a girl with him. I think it's Catriona McDonald,' said Cora. 'Looks like she's crying.'

'I bet he's heading for the hospital,' said Tam. 'That's the only reason for the horn and the hazard lights, I think.'

The van whizzed past, accelerating as it went.

'Aye, you are right, Tam,' Calum cried with more than a hint of enthusiasm. 'And that means we are needed, too. Come on, Cora. To the Lambretta!'

Eggy MacOnachie watched as the two journalists dashed across the street towards Calum's yellow scooter parked outside Allardyce the Baker's.

'Now I've seen everything,' he mused to himself. 'The press chasing the post.' Adjusting his binocular strap and setting his cap straight, he descended the steps to the quay.

The Macbeth roll-on, roll-off ferry, *Laird o' the Isles* loomed out of the morning mist and manoeuvred into the crescent-shaped harbour of Kyleshiffin. Then followed a bustle of practiced efficiency as the vessel was secured and the great landing doors slowly descended to allow the walking passengers to disembark before the cavalcade of traffic tumbled down the ramps onto the quayside.

Minutes later, DC Penny Faversham parked her three-door Mini Hatch in the available space in front of the clock tower as she had been instructed to do in Torquil's email. She switched off the engine, yawned and stretched her long legs as she prepared to wait for her new boss to come to meet her. She hadn't met the West Uist Inspector before, but had heard about him from Detective Superintendent Ross when she reported to Stornoway Police Station.

'He's used to running his own show over on West Uist,' he had told Penny in typical detective manner, as if he was giving a rundown on a suspect. 'He's into motorbikes, classic ones. Lives with his uncle, known as the Padre. Torquil is sometimes called Piper by his friends, on account of his being a champion bagpiper. He's a good copper, though you wouldn't know it from Superintendent Lumsden in the uniforms. He hates him with a passion, so it's as well that he was moved to the detective branch, which is where he started in Dundee.'

'A bit of a maverick, is he, sir?' Penny had asked.

He had shrugged non-committedly. 'He's an islander, so maybe that makes him a natural rebel. His fiancée, Lorna Golspie, is a sergeant in uniforms. You might have a chat with her. She'll give you the lowdown about the island.'

Which she did. Apart from making it abundantly clear in the nicest and most subtle manner possible that Torquil McKinnon was out of bounds, Sergeant Lorna Golspie had given Penny a complete outline of what to expect on West Uist. Lorna painted an attractive prospect, although she left Penny in no doubt about the weather.

'It's misty, rainy and windy,' she had told Penny. 'There isn't the traffic, the noise or the commotion. You might get bored after the big city life of Leeds.'

Despite all that, Penny was really looking forward to it. The mist that had surrounded the ferry for the last couple of hours had started to lift and what she could see of Kyleshiffin she liked already. She thought Harbour Street could be a picture postcard with its sea wall and harbour, its crescent of differently coloured shop-fronts and businesses, its old town clock and the big red spherical Second World War mine at the top of the steps leading down to the quay. Blessed with good eyesight, even at this distance she read that this relic of war had been converted into a collection box for the Shipwrecked Fishermen and Mariners Royal Benevolent Society.

The word 'shipwrecked' resonated with her. Although she had much to be thankful about in her career as a detective constable in Leeds, her relationship with Barry Winder-Thompson had almost literally been a shipwreck. A Royal Navy officer, he had spent six months to nine months at sea during every one of their three years together. With her own busy life she had thought they could cope with that. What she had not expected was to discover that he, a warfare officer, had been sleeping with the ship's medic. Apparently, she had not been the first of his conquests. Not so much a case of a girl in every port as one onboard as well.

Bastard!

Penny had wanted nothing more than to get away from Leeds with all its memories of his shore leaves and of his infidelity. When the opportunity of a job came up in the remotest place she could think of, she applied and was appointed. She had upped anchor and headed north by north west, first to Stornoway for a briefing and then to West Uist.

Wildlife — one of her passions —, plenty of fresh air, and time to lick her wounds and reflect, that's what Penny craved.

The *Laird o' the Isles* ferry had completed its function and loaded up with vans, lorries and a few cars, then manoeuvred out of the harbour heading out to open sea again. But still there was no sign of DI Torquil McKinnon.

A couple of men came up the steps from the quayside. Both were wearing caps, one dressed in a Macbeth ferries uniform and the other, an older man in a brown shop-coat, was carrying a briefcase. Penny got out of her car and crossed the road.

'Excuse me, I'm expecting a Detective Inspector McKinnon to meet me,' she said.

'Oh, it's Piper you want, is it? I'm Tam MacOnachie, the harbour master, and this is Willie Armstrong, the Macbeth representative.'

'And I'm also the local butcher,' Willie volunteered.

Penny smiled at them. She guessed that things happened at a snail's pace on the island and she had no problem with that. 'Is the police station nearby? I think he must have been held up.'

Tam MacOnachie clicked his tongue. 'He could be. I'm thinking we may have had one emergency already this morning.'

'A police matter?' Penny asked.

Tam shook his head doubtfully. 'More a postal problem.'

He gave her directions to Lady's Wynd and she duly returned to her car and got in.

'A postal problem is considered an emergency here?' she mused to herself with a satisfied smile. 'I think the pace of life on West Uist is going to suit me very well.'

Doctor Ralph McLelland was one of Torquil's oldest friends. He was the third generation of his family to minister to the local people of West Uist. After reading Medicine at Glasgow University he had embarked upon a career in forensic medicine, having gained a diploma in medical jurisprudence as well as the first part of his membership of the Royal College of Pathologists. His father's terminal illness had drawn him back to the island to take over the practice, which he had then run single-handedly for seven years. In that time, he gained his full pathology qualification, which along with his role as the police surgeon enabled him to perform occasional post-mortem examinations at the hospital. That, and all of the other tasks that fell to an island GP, like delivering babies and performing minor surgery, kept him busy most of the time.

Ralph had been about to start his morning surgery at the hospital when Torquil's call came in and he had to announce to the waiting room that he had to go, offering first to see anyone whose condition could not wait. Fortunately no one needed his immediate ministrations.

He was waiting with Lizzie Lamb, the charge nurse in charge of the hospital in the accident and emergency room, which doubled as their admitting unit. With her staff of two others Lizzie was kept busy. Indeed, no matter how many patients they had under her care, she was always busy. She could have six extremely ill patients in the hospital and beetle about, coping admirably, or just one and be run off her feet. But patient care never suffered or was in any way compromised. She just liked her patients to appreciate that the nursing life was a busy one. What everyone knew was that she was dependable and would be there for her patients no matter what.

Both Sister Lamb and Ralph McLelland knew Catriona McDonald and her divorced parents, Councillor Charlie and Bridget McDonald very well.

Catriona was a good kid in year S5 at Kyleshiffin Community Academy, as the Kyleshiffin School was now named. She was always smiling and much given to changing her hair colour. She was in her Highers year and wanted to be a nurse, so had actually done work experience at the hospital, both on the wards and shadowing Ralph in the odd surgery. It was a shock to see her in the state brought in by Stan Wilkinson.

When Calum Steele and Cora Melville came rushing in shortly after them, Sister Lamb had adroitly side-lined them with her stock, 'We're unable to comment until the patient has been assessed by the doctor and permission to speak to the press has been given.'

Like Torquil, Calum was one of Ralph's oldest friends. Indeed, as boys they had imagined themselves to be like the Three Musketeers when they were attending the Kyleshiffin School under Miss Bella Melville's watchful eye. Then they had grown up and gone their separate ways; Torquil to study law and become a police officer, Ralph to study medicine and Calum to throw himself into journalism. As a kid Calum had been nosy and persistent, but as a newspaperman he had the tenacity of a bulldog and the guile of a fox.

Ralph was grateful that Sister Lamb had protected him from the journalist duo so that he could focus on the emergency case, although he knew that they wouldn't be totally put off, so he told her to tell them that he would call if he was able to divulge anything later.

Diagnostically, Ralph had little doubt about Catriona's state of inebriation and her visual trouble.

'It's just misty smoke and bright flashes and sparks that I see,' Catriona had said, panic in her still slurring voice as he took her history. 'I … I can't breathe properly either.'

'I'm going to put up a drip soon and that'll help the breathing, Catriona. But first I need to know more. How much of this peatreek did you drink?'

'A lot, but not as much as Vicky, and nowhere near as much as Jamie.' She began trembling again and tears ran down her cheeks. She sniffed and panted. 'C-Can you get my sight back, Doctor? Ha-Have you told my folks yet?'

'The police have spoken to them and I understand that they are both on their way. I'll need to speak to them as soon as they get here.' He nodded to Lizzie who passed him an ophthalmoscope. 'Now, let me examine your eyes a bit closer. When I asked you how many fingers I was holding up you said you couldn't see anything, so I need to look inside your eyes. Sister Lamb is going to switch off the light and I'm going to shine this instrument into your eyes. It's like a torch. You won't feel anything.'

Sister Lamb doused the light and Ralph switched on the ophthalmoscope and leaned close to look through the series of lenses inside the instrument to assess the state of retina in each of Catriona's eyes.

A few moments later after the lights were switched on again, Ralph told her: 'We'll need to take some blood for tests, Catriona. Now, answer me honestly, did you take anything else? Any drugs of any sort? I need to know.'

'Just the whisky. Jamie brought it. We were … celebrating finishing our exams for the Highers.'

She began to sob and Ralph put a hand on her wrist.

'OK, Catriona. I'm going to go and talk with the eye specialist and the kidney specialist at Stornoway and once I have I'm going to start treating you. We're going to do our utmost to help you.'

Catriona sat back in alarm. 'K-Kidney specialist. There's nothing wrong with my kidneys is there, Doctor McLelland?'

This time Sister Lamb bent down and put a comforting arm about the youngster's shoulders. 'We're going to look after you, petal. Don't you worry.'

'That's right, Catriona,' Ralph said. 'The whisky you had must have been tainted with methanol, that's —'

'— methyl alcohol, I know that from chemistry,' Catriona said. 'But Jamie said it was good stuff and totally safe.'

'Aye, well, clearly it wasn't. I think it must have been illicit whisky. We'll need to transfer you to Stornoway where they can dialyse you to get the poison out of your system. It can damage your kidneys and we need to make them safe.'

He left her in Sister Lamb's care while he went to his office to phone the Western Isles Hospital on Stornoway. Before he reached the end of the corridor he picked up Torquil's call.

'Ah, Torquil, the very man. I'm waiting for Charlie and Bridget McDonald to show up. I'm going to need their permission to treat Catriona.'

'That's partly why I'm ringing. Ewan has just talked to them separately. He said you should know that there is friction between them.'

'Aye, they are divorced. They're both patients of mine, so I'm aware that there are — issues.'

'And I'm afraid I'll need you up here pronto to certify young Jamie. We're stymied until you do and the Scene Examiner gets here.'

Ralph was used to pressure. 'As soon as I can afford to leave my live patient, I'll be there, Torquil.'

'So what is your verdict with Catriona?'

'Well, I'm virtually one hundred per cent sure it's methanol poisoning. We're taking blood for testing, but I can't wait for the results. I'll need to treat her as soon as possible before permanent damage sets in. I'm just about to check in with the specialists on Stornoway, but I'm pretty sure I know what I'll need to do.'

'Can you get her sight back?'

'It'll be touch and go. She's lost her pupillary reaction and her optic discs inside her eyes are all congested. She has what we call optic neuritis.'

Calum and Cora were just about to get on the scooter to return to the office when Charlie McDonald's Mercedes careered into the car park. A moment later the local councillor and his ex-wife Bridget McDonald got out and flounced towards the main door.

'Ah, Charlie, could I have a word?' Calum ventured.

'No comment, Calum!' came the curt reply from the councillor.

'Come on, Charlie,' snapped Bridget, giving Calum and Cora a disdainful look as she walked quickly past them. 'Have you not dithered enough, you bloody idiot.'

Calum was about to follow until Cora put a hand on his arm. 'I think we ought to wait for Doctor McLelland's call this time, Calum. It sounds as if things are fraught enough right now.'

Calum tisked and absently reached into his anorak pocket for the bag containing his half-eaten mutton pie. He unwrapped it. 'You see, the journalist's life is never easy, Cora. We of the fourth estate are the most misunderstood of all the professions. People consider us pariahs, busybodies, when all we aim to do is keep people up to date and informed. Then when they need us —' He gave a short laugh and took a munch on his pie.

Cora smiled and linked her arm through his. 'You're no pariah, Calum Steele. I think you're the bee's knees. Come on, it's been a long night.' She covered her mouth and gave an exaggerated yawn and then winked. 'I could just do with a nap on the office couch while we wait for the news from Ralph.'

Calum beamed and took her hand. 'It's back to the office for us then. We must cater to the needs of the Press and of the journalists.'

CHAPTER SIX

Ralph had a rather brisk consultation with Charlie McDonald and his ex-wife Bridget. Charlie had gone in on the offensive, backed up immediately by Bridget.

'What the hell is happening here, Dr McLelland? How come Catriona's been admitted?'

'Why did PC McPhee say it was an emergency, Doctor?' Bridget enquired.

Her ex-husband jabbed the air in front of him. 'I need answers and I'm warning you, if I'm not satisfied, I'll be straight on the phone to my solicitor.'

Ralph adroitly deflected their questions and tried to assuage their anxiety as best he could, at the same time leaving them in no doubt that the situation was urgent.

'Who was she up there with?' Charlie McDonald asked forcefully.

'I don't have the information and I'm not at liberty to say anyway. That is for the police to tell you.'

'Look here, if my daughter —!'

Bridget McDonald put a restraining hand on her ex-husband's arm. 'Charlie, be quiet, can you not understand what Dr McLelland is telling you, you big lummox? He needs to start treatment right away to save her sight.' Shaking her head in exasperation, she held out her hands for the consent form attached to a clipboard. 'Let me sign and let's get on with it.' As she did so the tears started to trickle down her cheeks. 'Please, Ralph, do whatever you have to do.'

'I will. I've just spoken to the consultant ophthalmologist and the kidney specialist at Stornoway. As soon as I've initiated treatment and I'll get her over to the Western Isles Hospital for dialysis.'

Charlie McDonald grabbed his arm, tears welling up in his eyes. 'She's my wee girl, Ralph. Do what you must.'

After initiating treatment and seeing some improvement in the clinical condition of her eyes, albeit accompanied by progressive deepening of her inebriation, Ralph left Catriona in the capable hands of Lizzie, while he arranged the air ambulance to transfer her to Stornoway, along with her mother.

Then he left in the Kyleshiffin Cottage Hospital ambulance, which was actually a fairly old camper van that had been donated by a former laird and adapted at public cost.

He parked below the pillbox and jumped out with his old Gladstone bag swinging from his hand.

'Thanks for coming, Ralph,' Torquil called down from above, where he and Morag were waiting. 'This is a hell of a business and we've not enough folk on the ground.'

'Any news on Vicky Spiers?' the doctor asked as he ducked under the police tape.

'The twins are out looking for her, but unfortunately they haven't found any tracks. Can you come and take a look at Jamie Mackintosh?'

Although it was clear to Ralph that the youngster was dead, he was too professional to skimp on his examination to certify death. By the light of the lantern inside the pillbox he felt the body for pulses, listened with his stethoscope for a heartbeat and breath sounds, but found none.

'His pupils are fixed and dilated,' he said over his shoulder to Torquil and Morag. He gently lifted the head and turned it to the right and left. 'No automatic movement of the eyes, they move in unison with the head, so that is a positive doll's sign. And there is no blink response if I touch the eyeball, meaning no corneal reflex.'

Reaching into his Gladstone bag he drew out his ophthalmoscope and spent some time examining the inside of each eye through it. 'There is cattle-trucking all over.'

'What's that mean, Ralph?' Torquil asked.

'It means that the blood in the retinal blood vessels have lots of little bubbles in them. It makes the vessels look like lines of cattle-trucks.'

'Does that tell us anything?'

'Just that he's dead. Gas is released from the blood after death as tiny bubbles.'

'What about rigor mortis?' Morag asked.

'It's developing. So, I am afraid that I can certify that life is extinct.'

'How long has he been dead, can you tell us?'

'Some hours, that's as much as I can say. It will be a Procurator Fiscal case and then a forensic post-mortem. That's out of my remit, though.'

'Has he inhaled vomit, do you think?' Morag asked.

'Possible, but the post-mortem will tell. He reeks of booze and from all the facts it is likely that he had a convulsion. He could have inhaled vomit as a result of that and asphyxiated.' He rose to his feet, winding his stethoscope up. 'So, I suspect that it was death from a convulsion and an overdose of methanol. That's methyl alcohol. One thing that would be worth doing and which would help the forensics and the pathologist would be for me to take blood now. The longer you leave it the more inaccurate the readings can be because of post-mortem changes. Shall I do that? It would need to be your decision.'

'Please, go ahead, Ralph,' Torquil told him. 'Then I'd better go and find his father to tell him the bad news. The trouble is that Ewan hasn't been able to contact him yet.'

'And someone had better go and see Vicky's parents,' said Morag with a sigh. 'Ewan contacted them to say that we're looking for her. Her mum wanted to come up and search herself, but he told her to stay and look after her husband in case she turns up there. Poor Brock Spiers can't walk, of course, after his accident. He's in a wheelchair and his wife Jeannie spends her time looking after him. They must be going frantic.'

'Better get Wallace or Douglas back here to look after the site, Morag,' Torquil replied. 'Now that Ralph has confirmed death you and I need to get back and get onto the Procurator Fiscal. We badly need more folk up here to look for Vicky and we need the Scene Examiner as soon as possible.' He looked at his watch. 'And for starts I'll need to get the new DC onto the job.'

Ewan had been busy telephoning round various people as he followed the instructions given to him by Morag. He had still been unable to locate Jamie Mackintosh's father, which troubled him considering the enormity of the situation. It didn't surprise him though, as Angus Mackintosh was well known for going off on benders ever since his wife had died three years before. Young Jimmy Mackintosh had virtually brought himself up.

The bell went off as the outer door of the station opened and Stan Wilkinson came in carrying a parcel and a wad of mail. Gone was his ready smile, replaced by a glum and shocked expression.

'You'll know all that's happened, Ewan?' he asked as he deposited the parcel and the mail on the counter.

'I cannot say how sad I am about this, Stan. It's a tragedy, losing a young island lad like that. Morag told me you took Catriona McDonald to the hospital.'

'I did, and I left her in the doctor's care. She was in a right state, Ewan. I didn't know how to comfort her. I just drove as fast as I could.' He leaned his elbows on the counter and cupped his bearded chin in his hands. 'Any news on the third teenager?'

'We're looking for her.' Ewan shivered. 'Let's hope she's OK.'

Stan sighed and stood upright again with a sigh. 'It looks like your murder shoes have arrived.'

Ewan opened and unwrapped the parcel to reveal a large shoebox. He opened it and pulled out two heavy brown lace-up boots, with additional leather wraparound straps and buckles above the ankles. They had been specially made with four inch steel blades protruding from the front of the toes.

Stan whistled. 'Wow! I see why you call them murder shoes. May I have a closer look? I've never seen anything like them.'

Ewan shrugged and handed them over for the postman to inspect.

The bell went as the outer door opened and a tall woman stepped inside. She was about five ten with auburn hair cut in a short natural style. She was wearing smart jeans, trainers and a light blue quilted waterproof jacket. Ewan thought he had never seen anyone so pretty in real life.

He put on his customary welcoming smile. '*Madainn mhath*, a good morning to you. Can I help you, miss?'

She smiled and advanced to the counter, nodding at Stan before turning her attention to Ewan. 'I'm DC Penny

Faversham,' she said, showing him her warrant card. 'I was supposed to meet DI McKinnon when I got off the ferry, but somehow he —' she shrugged and stowed her warrant card in a shoulder bag. 'He didn't show.' She gave a nervous little laugh. 'Could be the story of my life. Men not showing, I mean.'

Ewan wanted to say he found that hard to believe, but his natural shyness prevented the words from coming. Instead, he raised his hands apologetically.

'Pleased to meet you, DC Faversham. I'm Constable Ewan McPhee. The thing is we've had an emergency this morning.' He leaned closer and spoke in hushed tones. 'Three teenagers had been out drinking dirty alcohol all night. One's dead, one's missing and one's been taken to hospital. The boss is still up at the scene.'

Penny gasped. 'That's terrible!' She turned to Stan who was still holding one of the boots and rubbing the blade between his fingers and thumb. 'That's a lethal looking boot you have there,' she said.

Stan looked up at her with a start, his face like a frightened rabbit caught in the headlights of a car. Then, as if suddenly snapping out of a trance he looked down at the boot and hastily handed it back to Ewan as if it had suddenly become electrified. He stood staring awkwardly at Penny.

'I'm sorry, it's been a hell of a morning and when you said that word "lethal" — well, it gave me the willies.' He ran a hand over his beard and pointed at the door. 'I'd better be on my way, though. I'm still nowhere near finished my round.' And he abruptly turned and headed for the exit.

Once he had gone Penny pointed at the boot in Ewan's hands. 'What is that? Why has it got a blade sticking out of it?'

'Oh, these are my murder shoes.' Then seeing her eyebrows rise quizzically: 'Sorry, we call them that in the hammer-throwing fraternity. The proper name for them is hammer boots. We dig them into the ground when we throw the hammer, you see. I was explaining that to Stan, because he's English like you and didn't understand about the highland hammer.'

Penny was still looking puzzled.

'Are you OK, Penny? I mean, I hope it's OK to call you Penny?'

She shivered and then smiled. 'Sorry, I just had a strange sense of déjà vu. It was something about your murder shoes.'

'Maybe it was because we've had this death?' Ewan suggested. Then, raising the counter flap: 'Come on through. We'll have a good mug of strong tea while we wait for the boss to come back.'

'Have I got an office somewhere?' Penny asked doubtfully.

'Oh aye, it's — er — not very big, but I think it will have all you need,' Ewan said, opening a door next to Torquil's office to reveal what was once literally a broom cupboard. 'No window, I'm afraid, but you have a desk, filing cabinet, computer and a bookcase for your files.' He went in and clicked on an old fashioned green-shaded desk lamp. 'I went out and bought this to make up for the lack of a window. It sort of gives it a real detective feel, I think.' He beamed at her and added, 'I was tempted to get a big magnifying glass to leave on the desk, but thought that was maybe going too far.'

Penny was not overly impressed by the size of the office space, but she couldn't help being soothed by the big constable's smile and his almost melodic island accent.

Calum and Cora had gone back to the *West Uist Chronicle* offices in something of a hurry. In fact, 'newspaper offices' was a rather grandiloquent title, for although there was a large printed sign attached to the wall beside the door, the offices consisted of two floors, both of which had been used exclusively by Calum, until the happy day that Cora Melville, the great niece of Miss Bella Melville, Calum's old teacher, had walked into the office and into his life.

The actual news office itself, where Calum interviewed people and took orders for photographs that appeared in the paper, occupied the first room on the ground floor, with the archives of back issues in the room at the back. Upstairs was where the actual work took place. At the front was the room with a cluttered old oak desk where Calum wrote his articles on a vintage Mackintosh computer or on his spanking new laptop. Sitting between the two computers was a dusty old Remington typewriter, which served no real purpose other than to help him feel the part of a writer. In his mind he had been touched with the literary genius of Hemingway, the incisive mind of Sir Arthur Conan Doyle and the investigative journalism skills of Woodward and Bernstein.

The rest of the room was occupied with his digital printing press, paper and stationery supplies, and in the corner was the space where he stacked the next issue of the newspaper ready for distribution. Across the landing was a larger room which had been divided up to form kitchenette, a shower, a toilet, and a space with a room containing a battered old settee and a camp bed, which Calum used to use when he was either working late or when he felt too inebriated to return home. As the editor, printer and sole reporter of the paper he used to work flexible hours, his only rule being that however he managed it he would produce a paper every Tuesday and

Friday. Sometimes he even produced extra editions, which he called 'specials' when there was something of significant newsworthiness that he felt the good folk of West Uist needed to know about.

When Cora joined him as his chief reporter and introduced new technology, he had forked out for a new desk and computer for her and the *West Uist Chronicle* hit cyberspace, with its own website and a digital edition for those readers who had embraced social media.

'You really are the most amazing man, Calum Steele,' Cora trilled as she and Calum lay ensnared together in post-coital somnolence.

'And you are the most —' he began, only to be interrupted by his mobile phone suddenly ringing. 'That'll be Ralph,' he said, clicking it onto speaker mode. '*West Uist Chronicle*. Is that you, Ralph?'

'No, Calum, it's me — Torquil. And I need your help.'

The editor swung his stocky legs over the side of the camp bed and sat up. 'Is it about Catriona McDonald? Me and Cora saw her being taken into the hospital. Ralph was going to call me with news when he was able. I saw Charlie and Bridget, but they were too distressed to talk and I didn't press them.'

Torquil fleetingly told him about the three teenagers.

'That's awful news, Torquil. Jamie used to be one of my delivery lads before he started studying for his Highers. I knew it must be something serious with Catriona, what with her being brought in by Stan Wilkinson in the post van. He was driving along Harbour Street in the mist like a bat out of hell.'

'Aye, well, Ralph is arranging the transfer for Catriona to the Western Isles Hospital in Stornoway.'

'And Vicky Spiers?'

'We can't say too much yet to the public, but we badly need help. That's why I can't go to television or the radio. It's going to take time that we haven't got to get extra officers over from Lewis, so I need islanders up at the old pillbox on Harpoon Hill to search for Vicky Spiers. That's why I need your network.'

'The *West Uist Chronicle* is at your service, Piper. We've got emails from almost everyone on the island.'

'Well, maybe just email those folk who have suitable vehicles and who are physically able enough to go trekking across the moors.'

'And the beaches?'

There was a pause, then: 'Aye, anywhere the lassie could have wandered to. That includes anywhere she could have fallen. So far, the Drummond lads haven't found anything.'

'We'll get on the case straight away.'

'Thanks, pal. Just one thing, though. This is going to be incredibly sensitive, so please avoid sensationalism in the email.'

Calum opened his mouth to reply, but thought better of it when Cora dug her fingers into his chest. 'Understood. Let's just get the lassie home safe first.'

'Good man, Calum. I promise you I'll give you a full statement for the *Chronicle* as soon as I can. Just hold on until then.'

Cora kissed Calum's cheek as the phone went dead. She shot off the camp bed and skipped naked through to her desk and computer.

'I'll get the email list up and start weeding out the folk that won't be up to going on a search party. If you compose the email you want to send out to them then I'll make some tea and toast. I guess we'll need it.' As she sat down and moved her mouse to fire up her computer she beamed at him. 'I'm so proud of you for holding back, Calum.'

Calum waved his hand dismissively. 'Two more lessons in journalism for you, my wee darling. First, respect your sources and be mindful of their wishes. Secondly, sometimes a scoop doesn't have to appear in print. Everyone who receives the email we're going to send will appreciate that the news is coming from the *West Uist Chronicle.*'

Charlie McDonald had waited until Catriona was taken onto the air ambulance.

'She's going to be fine, Bridgie,' he began. 'I'll make sure —'

'I told you, don't call me that. And don't ever expect me to believe that you'll make sure of anything, you stupid man. If you'd been a half decent father, then —'

Catriona groaned on the stretcher. 'Mum … Dad … don't start, please,' she pleaded in a voice slurred from the ethanol she had been given.

Sister Lamb touched Charlie's arm. 'They need to go, Councillor McDonald. And Bridget, you'll need to get in now.'

Charlie had watched the helicopter rise swiftly into the air and head off as the rain started to come down. He pulled his jacket collar up and ran for his Mercedes. It was only when he got in and started up the ignition to put on his windscreen wipers that he noticed the Land Rover Defender parked outside the hospital grounds. Its lights flashed and then it started off and headed down the road, turning quickly uphill to head inland.

He followed at a discreet distance until he was well clear of Kyleshiffin and then accelerated to keep up with it. After a couple of miles the Land Rover turned off the road onto a track leading to the woods, one of their secret rendezvous spots. She always liked outdoor sex and told him that the risk of being discovered gave their relationship an extra frisson.

He drew into the small clearing where her vehicle was already parked. Esther Corlin-MacLeod was leaning against it. She was dressed elegantly in a quilted Barbour jacket over West Uist tweeds with knee high leather boots that looked more fashionable than necessary for a woodland walk. Indeed, with her ponytail protruding from under a stylish country cap she could have been a model on a shoot for *Country Life* rather than the entrepreneurial owner of a leading distillery and renowned Hebridean shooting estate.

'Is your daughter going to be all right, Charlie?' Esther asked as he got out and crossed to her. 'I've been worried about her since you rang me.'

'She's on her way to the Western Isles Hospital in Stornoway. Dr McLelland is sure she'll be OK, but he's still worried about her sight.'

Charlie's arms went around her waist and she snaked her arms about his neck and drew him to her as their lips met in a passionate kiss.

'Christ, are you sure you want to,' she muttered in his ear a few moments later as he ran his hands under her cashmere jumper, while she started to undo his belt.

'I bloody need it, Esther. Especially after the morning I've had.'

They were too preoccupied when both their mobile phones made sounds, indicating that they had each received a new email.

Helen Beamish had been busy all morning and still had a number of case files waiting her attention in the three baskets on her desk. She had dictated numerous letters and made many phone calls. Calum Steel's email had immediately grabbed her attention. The subject box read:

URGENT— MISSING TEENAGER — WE NEED YOU

She had read the short missive and immediately decided that action was needed. She pulled on her purple jacket from the back of her chair and alerted Hazie, her secretary, that she had received an email from the *West Uist Chronicle*, only to be told that both Hazie and Kathleen, Cameron Beamish's secretary had received the same email.

'I'd better get on with these reports, Helen,' Hazie said, 'but I'll text my Henry and get him to go out.'

'And I'd better stay and man Cameron's phone,' Kathleen said.

Helen was reaching for the reception door when it opened and her husband came in.

'Cameron!' she exclaimed. 'I wasn't expecting to see you back today. What's happened? You're supposed to be in Oban until tomorrow.' Cameron had been away resolving a case on the mainland.

Cameron smiled and shrugged. 'The other side decided to settle and so I caught the ferry and came back early to see my beautiful wife.'

'We've got an emergency, Cameron,' Helen interrupted. 'There's a missing teenager, Vicky Spiers, somewhere out on the moors by Harpoon Hill. The police have asked Calum Steele to get as many people as possible out looking for her, on the moors, on the beaches, anywhere. I've got to get going to help out.'

He looked down at his suit. 'I'd better pop home and get my wet weather clothes on. I'll follow you as soon as I change.'

'I'll see you later, then,' Helen said, kissing his cheek on her way out.

Once in her car she sat and thought for a moment before pulling out her phone and making a call.

Norma had finished breakfasts and went over all the management plans with her three team leaders, one for each floor of the home, before she was able to leave the Hydro. She drove her Fiat 500 over to Lochiel's Copse, where Robbie Ochterlonie lived alone in the log cabin that he had built himself. She knew that he liked his privacy and had aspirations to be a writer. A log cabin on the edge of woods with wildlife all around, he had told her, was a prime requisite to creative writing. Millie McKendrick was the first to tell her that he actually liked his solitude to drink his peatreek, the illicit whisky that he also peddled to some of the residents. Then Norma realised that the sweet odour that she was often aware of in the mornings was due to his drinking the night before.

His drinking was one of the things that Norma turned a blind eye to, but worried about in case the owners of the Hydro should find out. It would undoubtedly mean a scandal for the residential home and the sack for Robbie.

The cabin curtains were all still drawn shut when she got out of the car.

She knocked on the door and prayed that she'd hear him stirring inside. But she was greeted with silence.

She felt her heart quicken, for Doreen McGuire had implanted the fear that he might be unwell, possibly lying in a diabetic coma.

'Please, Robbie, just be drunk,' she whispered to herself as she tried the door handle. It was unlocked and opened easily.

'Robbie?' she called as she tentatively pushed the door open. 'It's me, Norma. Are you OK?'

The lights were still on and she saw Robbie lying face down in a pool of blood and vomit.

A scream threatened to burst forth, but she suppressed it and bent down to feel his neck for his carotid pulse.

There was none. His skin was cold and the tissues under it were already stiffening. Norma had seen enough dead bodies to know the worst. Robbie Ochterlonie was stone dead.

CHAPTER SEVEN

'Talk about a baptism of fire,' DC Penny Faversham said over a mug of Ewan's stewed tea late that night in the station restroom. 'Three teenagers go drinking overnight, one ends up dead, another is in hospital and the third is missing. And then that poor man dying suddenly.'

Ewan was pouring out tea for the other members of the West Uist police. 'It's not always like this,' he told her with a smile. 'It's normally a happy wee island.'

'I feel bad giving up on the search for Vicky Spiers,' said Wallace, spooning four sugars into his mug.

'We had to stop for the dark and the rain. It was starting to get dangerous for the searchers,' said Morag. 'We had a quarter of the island out and we didn't find any trace of her. We'll start again first thing in the morning though. Then we'll have uniformed officers from Lewis on the next ferry and we can be more organised.'

Torquil nodded. 'It shows how the island can work together. Calum and Cora did a sterling job mobilising folk to help with the search, even though we've been unsuccessful.'

'Do you think she could be dead, Piper?' asked Douglas Drummond.

Torquil felt a shiver run up and down his spine. 'I certainly hope not. I'm banking on her having found somewhere to crawl into and fall asleep.'

'Will we alert the television and radio tomorrow, Torquil?' asked Morag.

'Aye. I'll do that. And I promised Calum that I'd let him have a statement first thing. We have to play ball with him. It's going to be a busy day tomorrow for all of us.' He turned to DC Penny Faversham. 'I'm sorry that I had to give you a sudden death as your first job.'

She nodded and gave a wan smile. 'Dr McLelland said he couldn't issue a death certificate and so I had to contact the Procurator Fiscal's office, which I did. That's the second thing I've found quite different up here in Scotland. In England we call in unexpected deaths to the coroner.'

'Aye, they have a similar role,' Torquil replied. 'You'll have to read up on the differences between Scots law and English law. What was the other thing, Penny?'

She gave a short laugh. 'Language. I don't mean accents, but the Gaelic. Will I have to learn all this Gaelic? On the drive up the west coast to Oban I saw that all the road signs had both English and Gaelic names.'

'It is pretty controversial actually, Penny,' Morag explained. 'It has been a political issue for a few years, especially in the mainland parts where Gaelic is not spoken, or hasn't been spoken for centuries.'

'Here on West Uist you'll get by fine in English,' volunteered Ewan.

'What were your impressions about the scene, though?' Torquil asked. 'You'll need to write up your report in the morning, but just give me your overall impressions. You took photographs, didn't you?'

'I did. I know that the Senior Scene Examiner who came over from Lewis is going over the place again first thing in the morning, so I was careful not to disturb things more than I could help.'

She pulled out a pocket book from her waterproof jacket and opened it where she had made copious notes. 'The subject, known as Robbie Ochterlonie was a man of thirty-seven years, according to Dr McLelland's case notes. He is the manager of The Old Hydro Residential Home and he was found by Norma Ferguson, his assistant manager. She had gone there after she had finished supervising breakfasts for the residents, because he hadn't shown up this morning to take over his duties. He is a known type 1 diabetic, which means he uses insulin.'

'We used to know Robbie. He was a fisherman before he became a confirmed landlubber and found easier ways to make money running the Hydro,' said Wallace. 'He liked a drop of the hard stuff as well.'

'Not the real stuff either,' added Douglas. 'He was a peatreek man.'

'Peatreek?' Penny repeated.

'That's the name for illicit whisky, Penny,' said Torquil. 'The Irish have potcheen, the Americans have moonshine and in Scotland it is referred to as peatreek.'

Penny hummed interest. 'Well, there was certainly whisky around. He'd dropped a glass of it when he fell on his face. And there was an empty bottle that had rolled over to the wall.'

'What did Ralph think about the death?'

'He wouldn't commit himself. He seemed incredibly knowledgeable, though.'

'Ralph is a qualified pathologist as well as a GP,' Morag informed her.

'That explains his reticence then, I suppose. He said there were several possibilities.' She consulted her notes. 'First, he could have had a heart attack or stroke and collapsed. Second, he could have had a problem with his blood sugar, either hyperglycaemia, that's means a high sugar level, or hypoglycaemia, which is when it's too low. The latter would mean he'd overdone his insulin.'

'And was there any evidence of that?' Torquil asked.

Penny nodded. 'On his kitchen table there was a syringe and several bottles of insulin. They all seemed to be empty.'

Torquil nodded. 'The Senior Scene Examiner will record and tag everything.'

'I took a few photographs myself, boss. Dr McLelland didn't object,' said Penny, picking up her mobile phone and accessing her photos. She crossed the room and showed him the scene of the body lying face down, with the whisky glass and bottle nearby. Another was of the sitting room with an open roll-top desk and various notebooks and sheets of paper, one of the kitchen table with the syringe, medication and empty bottles of different types of insulin, then finally the empty bathroom, and the bedroom with a neatly made bed.

She went on: 'The other possibility was that he'd drunk himself senseless and fallen. Whichever it was, he seemed to have broken his nose and possibly also fractured his skull, according to Dr McLelland. A post-mortem will tell which.'

'That's a good job, Penny,' Torquil said. 'We'll review it all when we have the Scene Examiner's report and the results from the post-mortem.'

'There was something that did really concern me, though, boss,' she said, using the informal title for the first time.

'Tell us,' said Torquil.

'I interviewed Norma Ferguson, of course. She was also worried this morning that two of her care assistants hadn't shown up.'

'Did she say anything else? What were their names?'

'Vicky Spiers and Catriona McDonald.'

Torquil frowned. 'Well, we know where Catriona is and we know where she and Vicky were, but not where she is now. We better be ready to muster the search party at first light.' He took a hefty sip of tea. 'And the other search will be for Angus Mackintosh. I need to talk to him and give him the bad news as soon as possible. Anyone have any idea of where he could be?'

'I've tried everywhere, boss,' said Ewan.

Torquil nodded. 'Then I suggest we all sleep on it.'

To everyone's dismay the new day had not brought an improvement in the weather. If anything, the clouds had descended further, causing dense fog, and on the ground the mist was as thick as it had ever been. The weather forecast was for more of the same for the whole week.

Morag organised the search team at dawn. It consisted of the six uniformed police constables from Lewis, about forty islanders who had helped the day before and the Drummond twins. Ewan was left to man the station, and while Torquil wanted nothing more than to help, he had to contact the Procurator Fiscal and the labs on the mainland. As DC Penny Faversham had experience of attending scenes of death he sent her to work with the Senior Scene Examiner from Lewis.

Morag split the searchers into groups, each under the supervision of a uniformed police officer and gave them photocopied maps marked out with the areas that she wanted them to comb, using the cordoned off pillbox as the starting point to spread out from.

The Senior Scene Examiner had set up a tent with all the forensic kit needed and could be seen working, accompanied by Penny, both dressed in white crime suits.

Calum and Cora had gone out to Harpoon Hill to interview some of the searchers as they prepared a special edition of the *West Uist Chronicle* and recorded little video clippings for the newspaper's blog. Morag spotted them immediately and discouraged them from going near the police cordon tape. She promised that Torquil would brief them as planned when he was able to.

Ian Gillesbie, the Senior Scene Examiner was a forty-five-year-old man who had seen every imaginable crime scene and could not be flustered by anything. He detailed every step of what he was doing into a hands-free headset microphone recorder.

Penny watched and noted everything down, from the meticulous photographing of the body and the site, the taking of samples and the bagging and labelling of the bottles, packets and debris of the teenagers' overnight activity.

When finished he clicked it off and stood up to talk to Penny.

'A grim business, Detective Faversham. By the smell of the bottle it's alcohol related, probably methanol adulteration as you said. There doesn't seem to have been any sexual shenanigans going on among them. His clothes are relatively undisturbed, no love bites on his skin and no sign of used condoms.'

'Will it take long to get the samples tested?' Penny asked, lowering her mask.

'The lab will get the whisky bottle done straight away and see precisely what it contained, and they'll also check to see if the bottle itself can reveal anything. The bloods that Dr Ralph McLelland took we'll also get analysed quickly. As for the body, well, it will all depend on a post-mortem by the pathologist. I'm no doctor, but I'm wondering if this young man had an underlying medical condition.'

Penny nodded. 'I understand Dr McLelland also sent blood off from Catriona McDonald. It will be interesting to compare them.'

Ian clicked his tongue. 'Whoever supplied them with this stuff is going to be hot under the collar. I can't say I have any sympathy with them either. One young life snuffed out and another maybe maimed for life.'

Penny peeled back one of her gloves from the wrist and glanced at her watch. 'And a third teenager still to be found. Are we about finished up here? Because we have the other case to see. The boss wants me to assist you there, too.'

Ian bowed with a show of old world gallantry. 'I'll be as swift and efficient as I can. It's not often I get two separate jobs so close together. If the next is as your report suggests it will be a snip.'

Torquil's phone went off early that morning. To his surprise it was Dr Ralph McLelland.

'I think you'll be wanting to come down to the hospital, Piper. I've got Angus Mackintosh in the accident room. He's pissed as a newt and he's lost a lot of blood.'

'Does he know about Jamie?'

'He does. I thought it was my duty as his family doctor, especially as I had confirmed his death. He found it difficult to take in, of course, what with the booze he's had and the blood that he's lost.'

'So he'd been on a bender? Did he fall and injure himself?'

'Like Robbie Ochterlonie? Actually no, he hadn't. It's a strange tale, I'll fill you in when you come in. Anyway, I'd better go. I need to stitch him up. I'll have finished by the time you get here, so you can talk to him then.'

'Did he drive himself in?'

'No, it was our local good Samaritan once again. Stan Wilkinson delivered him in his Royal Mail van.'

Torquil was relieved that Ralph had broken the bad news to Angus Mackintosh. He did not know him well, but he had encountered him professionally on a few occasions in the past, mainly as a result of being drunk and disorderly. And on two occasions of common assault, both while under the influence of alcohol. Allowance had been made because he was a widower and a single parent. Ralph had passed on the information that he was not a habitual drinker, but more of a toper who went on binges when black depression overcame him. It was not an easy situation, since he refused the offer of antidepressants or counselling.

Ralph was entering his case notes as he told Torquil the details.

'Stan Wilkinson found him crawling up a track from one of the old crofts beyond the Wee Kingdom. He was drunk, confused and injured. He'd apparently been doing up a cottage and somehow put a nail-bolt through his thigh. It hit a blood vessel and he lost a lot of blood and passed out.'

'Had he been drinking?'

Ralph shrugged. 'I don't know if he had before the accident, but he told Stan he came round, used a belt as a tourniquet and then drank near a bottle of whisky to get the courage to pull the bolt out. He couldn't just pull it out, though, he had to cut it out, which is why I've had to clean the wound up, stitch it and leave a drain in. Anyway, he collapsed, woke up hours later and dragged himself out, hoping to see someone.'

'Why did he not take his vehicle.'

'He couldn't remember where it was and he doubted that he could get in it, let alone drive.'

Angus himself virtually reiterated the whole story when Torquil saw him in his bed in a room on his own. His right leg was heavily bandaged and a drainage tube hung from it over the side of the bed.

'It isn't real,' Angus said, his face buried in his hands. 'My boy Jamie, he's doing his Highers. He's a clever lad and he'll be off to uni soon.'

'I'm so sorry, Mr Mackintosh. But we will need you to identify his body later this morning.'

Angus slowly raised his head and stared at Torquil. His eyes were bloodshot and tears had moistened his stubbly cheeks. He took a deep breath and nodded his head. Then: 'And the other two? Vicky and Catriona, was it?'

Torquil put a hand on the man's shoulder. 'I'm afraid that Catriona has been transferred to the Western Isles Hospital in Stornoway. She's got visual problems and is being dialysed.'

'Dialysed? What does that mean?'

'It's a treatment to use a machine to work like the kidneys to clear the poison out of her system.'

'And Vicky?'

'She's missing and we're searching for her.'

'Good God! This is an island. How can you still be looking for her?'

'We were looking for you too, Angus.'

'What did you say about poison?' he asked, shaking his head as if to clear his mind.

'We believe they'd been drinking peatreek with a high quantity of methyl alcohol in it.'

Angus's jaw muscles tightened and he clenched his fists. 'I'll find out who gave them it and I'll bloody kill them.'

His eyes blazed with fury for some moments and then the enormity of what had happened seemed to dawn on him again and he dissolved into tears. He dropped his head and his sobs racked his body.

'I ... I've lost them both, now. It's not fair! it's not fair.'

Again Torquil put a hand on his shoulder and waited until his sobbing settled. 'Angus, as soon as the Scene Examiner has completed his investigation I'll arrange for you to see Jamie to identify him.'

Angus nodded his head but said nothing.

Later, over the phone, Torquil gave Calum the full rundown on the three teenagers and the current state of the investigation.

'The Stornoway Coastguard Rescue helicopter has joined the search, scouring the sea and the coastline,' Torquil told Calum. 'Hopefully, with so many people involved, it will not be long before we find her or some track that will help us.'

'And dogs?' Calum asked. 'I contacted the Strathshiffin estate's gamekeeper, Guthrie Frazer and he said that he and his underkeeper would turn out with their dogs.'

'Aye, Guthrie was out yesterday, but I guess it was too wet to pick anything up. Rain dampens the smell, of course. Let's hope for a different result today.'

'Cora is going to interview the Spiers, since she knows them and already has a good rapport with them.'

'We have to be as reassuring as we can, without being unrealistic, Calum. We can't promise them anything other than we'll do our best to find her unharmed.'

'Aye, Cora's intelligent and sensitive, so don't worry.' Then he said what Torquil was dreading to hear: 'As for me, I'll be having a chat with Angus Mackintosh.'

'Not yet, Calum, please. The Senior Scene Examiner has only just taken all the samples and assessed the scene, and Ewan has arranged for Allan Moorhouse the undertaker to bring the body back to the hospital mortuary. We'll be able to get Angus to formally identify him there, before we transfer the body to Lewis for the post-mortem.'

'In that case, I'll leave it a day or so. And will you be talking to television or radio?'

Torquil knew that Calum wanted to be assured of his scoop. 'I'll have to soon, Calum. This is too tragic a happening to delay, you know that.'

'I'd better get back to the office and start writing then. How long will you give me?'

'An hour, then I'll be calling in to BBC Scotland.'

The phone went dead as Calum switched off. Torquil heaved a sigh of relief. Clearly, Calum hadn't heard about the death of Robbie Ochterlonie and he saw no reason to inform him as he'd find out soon enough. Besides, he had enough to fill several newspaper editions as it was.

Vicky Spiers slowly felt herself rise to consciousness after what seemed like hours of a stupor that she could not waken from. Her head hurt more than she ever thought possible. Worse than the pain, though, was the nausea.

Where am I? she thought. *Where are the others?*

Then she realised that she could not see, nor even open her eyes. Something was holding them shut and it hurt to even attempt to move her eyelids.

Oh God! What's happened to me? I'm sitting on a chair, I think, but I can't move a muscle. My hands! They're tied behind me!

There was not a sound. No breathing. No Talking. Nothing.

Panic set in when she tried to open her mouth, only to find the same constriction about her mouth and face. Something had been wrapped around her head, over her eyes and over her mouth. The nausea welled up inside her and she felt bile in the back of her throat.

No! No! No! Don't be sick.

Her fear-stricken mind tried to piece together her last memories, but it was all a haze.

Jamie! Catriona! The old pillbox.

A dim recollection of waking up somewhere outside came to her. It was misty and it made her cough and splutter. She was stumbling around and seemed to hit a track of some sort. Then she heard something, but what was it?

Then she recalled an explosive pain in the back of her head and felt herself hurtling forward, diving into a deep dark pool of unconsciousness.

And then waking up now — in hell.

CHAPTER EIGHT

Early the next morning, over a breakfast of Archie Reid's famous West Uist smoked kippers, Torquil and his uncle watched the early morning Scottish TV news on the small television set on top of the fridge. Kirsty Macroon was interviewing the political editor about the fallout over a revelation about an affair between two MSPs at Holyrood. As she finished a picture of West Uist appeared in the backdrop.

'Here it comes,' Torquil said.

'And now we turn to West Uist where a human tragedy has occurred. Three teenagers seem to have been experimenting with alcohol, with tragic consequences. Sadly, there has been a fatality.'

She gave a brief account of the event, identifying Jamie Mackintosh as the deceased and asking for consideration for the family. Then: 'I spoke to Detective Inspector Torquil McKinnon last night when the search for the missing teenager, Vicky Spiers was halted due to darkness. I asked him how the tiny police force on the island was coping.'

Torquil's voice, slightly distorted due to the telephone connection was accompanied by subtitles.

'We are doing everything in our power to locate Vicky Spiers. We had the Stornoway Coastguard Rescue helicopter out all afternoon and have drafted in more officers from Lewis. As well as that the *West Uist Chronicle* assisted us by putting out a request for islander volunteers to help us, with an amazing response. We have split into several teams and are methodically searching the island in a scientific manner.'

The picture turned to Kirsty Macroon. 'That is good to hear that the community is pulling together, but how concerned are you for her safety? I mean, it is now two days and for a youngster to be out alone in the weather that you get over on West Uist, well, that is worrying. Could you comment on that?'

'It is alarming of course, but we hope that she has found shelter somewhere. We have to be positive and we will be starting the search again at first light. We will find her.'

As Kirsty Macroon went on to another news item Torquil sighed and switched off the television with the remote control. He harrumphed. 'I only wish I was that confident. Morag will be out there coordinating the search party again. We just hope the weather doesn't get too bad, or we have trouble. I'd better get off as I have a stack of things to do at the station. Allan Moorhouse the undertaker took the two bodies across to Lewis on the late ferry and the post-mortem on Jamie is scheduled for first thing this morning at the Western Isles Hospital in Stornoway. I phoned Lorna and asked her to attend on our behalf.'

'Is Superintendent Lumsden allowing her?'

'He is. Considering the nature of the event he could hardly refuse. And I've also asked her to visit Catriona McDonald while she's at the hospital.'

'She'll not relish the post-mortem, I am thinking.'

'That's what she said, but she's been to many before so she'll cope. In a way it's been just as well for us that she's stationed there at the moment.'

'What about poor Robbie Ochterlonie? That's another tragedy we were not expecting.'

'Accidents happen though, especially when alcohol is involved.' Torquil rose from his seat and crossed to the door. 'What are your plans? Golf?'

The Padre tisked and looked apologetic. 'As a matter of fact I will be playing a few holes despite this situation on the island. I have an appointment with one of my flock, who needs my support. He wasn't quite ready to unburden himself when we last met, but I think this time he might.'

Torquil nodded. He knew better than to ask more, for his uncle was always loath to breach a confidence.

Ewan was busy writing up reports when the bell rang alerting him that someone had entered the vestibule. A moment later Stan Wilkinson popped his head round the corner.

'Ah, Stan, *madainn mhath*,' Ewan greeted. 'Have you time for a cup of tea?'

Stan came in with a handful of mail. He shook his head as he handed the bundle to Ewan. 'No, I've got a busy round today. I thought I'd call in early and ask if there was more news on the missing girl? Or about Catriona, the one I took to the hospital?'

'The search is on again this morning for Vicky. As for Catriona, Inspector McKinnon will be checking today.'

The postman pursed his lips. 'Did you hear that I found another casualty, too.'

'Angus Mackintosh! Aye, you did another good job there, Stan. The poor man, I cannot imagine what he must be going through.'

'He was not in a good state when I picked him up.'

'These things shouldn't happen on a wee island like West Uist, Stan. But still, we have to do what we can to find Vicky and just hope that Catriona McDonald recovers fully.'

Stan tugged pensively on his beard. Then with a shrug and a wry smile he asked: 'How are the murder shoes? I bet you'll have been out trying them out.'

Ewan shook his head. 'Not yet. To tell the truth, I have neither the time nor the inclination until we find Vicky. They're still under the counter here in their box.'

Stan gave a short laugh. 'Could I have a look at them again? I got a bit flummoxed when your detective came in. What did you say her name was?'

'DC Penny Faversham,' Ewan replied. 'Sure you can look, but mind the blades, they're meant for digging into the ground.' He bent to pick up the box and placed it on the counter.

Stan opened the box and took one out. He held it up to examine it and ran a finger along the blade.

'Maybe I'll see you practising with them another morning when I'm on my round,' he said, handing it back.

'That's quite likely, Stan,' Ewan replied as he stowed it back in the box, 'but as I said, I've no appetite for it at the moment. I have to say that it's frustrating for me having to man the phone here instead of being out there on the search with everyone else.'

'But you're needed here, mate,' Stan replied. He shoved his hands in the pockets of his shorts. 'Well, I'd better be off. Who knows, I may spot the girl on my rounds. They always say things come in threes.' He turned to go, then stopped and snapped his fingers. 'Oh, I almost forgot. Can I get my phone back now? It's here, I suppose?'

Ewan held out his hands apologetically. 'I don't know where it is, Stan. Sergeant Driscoll had it, I know that. I'll ask her when I see her. Do you need it urgently?'

Stan waved his hand dismissively and opened the door. 'No, it's not urgent, don't worry about it. I'll keep popping in until I catch the sergeant.'

Five minutes later Ewan was about to make a phone call when the bell announced another visitor to the station. This time the sound of several dogs barking preceded the opening of the door.

Ewan swallowed hard and put the phone down as an elderly lady dressed in a heavy raincoat and an ill-fitting panama hat with a prodigiously large shoulder bag bustled in with five dogs, but only three of them on leads. A rather disdainful looking German Shepherd and a zestful West Highland terrier came in ahead of three boisterous puppies of indeterminate breeds that were straining on their leads. Annie McConville, a widowed lady of seventy-odd years was something of a local celebrity known throughout the Western Isles both for her vague eccentricity and for the dog sanctuary that she ran single-handedly.

'Ah, Ewan McPhee, the very man I wanted to see,' she said, beaming up at him.

'Mrs McConville, those are three lively wee pups you have there.'

'Aye, well, I had to go and bring them back from Oban. It is a crime that people abandon poor wee fellows like these.' She opened her coat and produced treats from a pocket of the cheese-cloth dress she was wearing underneath and distributed them to the pack. 'I'll get them trained up and hopefully we'll get them all good homes. I know you'll be busy what with the search going on for that poor girl, Vicky Spiers, so I just wanted to tell you that I can put four of my dogs at your disposal. Not these wee puppies, but Zimba and Sheila here, and Walt and Nero at home. I can bring them up in my Hillman Imp.'

Ewan smiled. 'I'll give Morag Driscoll a call right away. I'm sure she'll welcome you. We want all the help we can get.'

While he was on the phone DC Penny Faversham came in. Immediately, Ewan smiled at her and raised his other hand in greeting. Penny returned the wave and dropped down on one knee to greet the puppies.

'What have we here. They're all gorgeous,' she enthused as she allowed them to lick her hands. 'Are they all yours, Mrs—?'

'McConville, Annie McConville. Aye, they are all mine, for now. That is until I can find good homes for these three. Zimba and Sheila here are part of my family, though.'

Ewan finished on the phone. 'That's all fine, Annie. Sergeant Driscoll welcomes the help. She's got Guthrie Finlay and his dogs from the Strathshiffin estate, but the more the better. If you could drive up to the pillbox on Harpoon Hill and park on the roadside then she'll meet you there. She'll allocate one dog each to three of the Lewis bobbies and you work with either Zimba or Sheila.'

'It'll need to be Sheila,' Annie replied. 'Zimba will get on with anyone, but Sheila can be a law to herself if she's out of my sight.'

'Mrs McConville, this is DC Penny Faversham,' Ewan introduced.

Penny stood up and shook the older woman's hand.

'Mrs McConville runs a dog sanctuary,' Ewan continued. 'What she doesn't know about dogs isn't worth knowing.'

'Oh, away with you, Ewan McPhee. Or rather, away we go, I'd better get back and pick up Walt and Nero. Good day to you, DC Faversham.'

Once they were alone the two officers beamed at one another.

Be careful, you fool, Penny silently chided herself. *You came here to get away from Leeds and bloody Lieutenant Barry Winder-Thompson. PC Ewan McPhee is a hunk, but frying pans and fires rings a bell.*

Ewan was about to speak when Penny's expression abruptly changed and she became serious and professional.

'I'd better get going, too. Lots of calls to make,' she said. 'No time for loose chat.'

She lifted the counter flap and let herself through.

'Would you like some tea?' Ewan called after her, his tone hopeful. 'I could bring it in.'

Penny went straight to her office and opened the door. 'Maybe later,' she said, gracing him with the slightest of smiles before swiftly closing the door behind her.

Morag had been trying to keep positive and maintain an air of professional calm in the face of mounting concern that none of the teams had found any sign of Vicky Spiers.

The pillbox was still cordoned off and the entrance had been closed with a large tarpaulin.

Standing outside and scanning the area with binoculars she peered as far as she could into the fog and mist and dimly saw some members of the teams, some deep in the moor, others climbing the Corlin foothills. From time to time she heard one of the dogs bark as the Coastguard search and rescue helicopter passed overhead.

'I tell you, Helen, I'll be relieved when we find some clue as to where she is,' she said to the local solicitor, standing beside her, drinking tea that she had poured from the tea urn that was part of the library van's accoutrements.

'We all will, Morag. She's a good kid. I've known her folks pretty well since Brock had his accident and I handled his claim for compensation against the Glen Corlin estate. It didn't make me popular with Esther Corlin-Macleod for a couple of years after all the compensation she had to pay out.'

'That was a bad accident. It shook the whole island.'

'It was an accident that should never have happened, Morag. Crushed under a whisky barrel that hadn't been stabilised on its stack. He was lucky he wasn't killed. As it was he suffered a broken spine that left him paraplegic. It was negligence pure and simple. Still, what's a couple of million compared to being able to walk.'

'I suppose you can make enemies when you practice law,' Morag said, lowering her binoculars and looking at her friend.

'It depends what type of law you practice. Beamish's is a small old-fashioned firm so we handle all types of cases, from divorce to commercial and criminal. I do most of the wills, power of attorney, personal injury and property cases, while Cameron does the criminal law and divorce and separation work. Actually, he makes more enemies than me.'

'Cameron does quite a bit of travelling, too, doesn't he?'

'Yes, to the mainland. He has to go round the courts in most of the cities, lucky fellow. I just get to go to Romania to see my sister in Bucharest when I occasionally need to escape from the island. She's married to a professor of chemistry at the university.'

Morag gave a wry smile. 'I've never even been to England. Still Helen, we appreciate you joining the search when you have a busy practice to run.'

'It's the least I can do. Cameron came yesterday, as you know, but he's holding the fort today.' She drained her coffee. 'I needed that, but now I'd better get back.' She squeezed Morag's elbow and gave a reassuring nod. 'I'm sure we'll find her.'

'Let's just hope that the rain holds off, though visibility seems to be getting poorer.' Morag's mobile phone went off and as she looked at the screen she saw that it was a call from Wallace Drummond.

'Morag, we've found a trainer in bracken by the old Strathshiffin road. Annie McConville's dog found it.'

'Is it just the one trainer?'

'Aye, just the one. It's still got its laces tied and it looks as if it came off in the mud.'

'Can you send me a picture, mark off the area and then bring it here?'

'Will do,' he replied and rang off.

'Good news?' Helen asked.

'We've found a trainer, but whether it's good news or not I don't know.'

Kathleen Peterson had locked the door to Beamish solicitors as soon as Hazie, Helen Beamish's secretary left for lunch. Cameron was working in his office, his sleeves rolled up and his tie loosened about his neck. When Kathleen pushed open the door and strolled in he pretended that he hadn't heard her and went on working.

'It's time to take a break, you naughty legal owl,' she whispered as she approached his desk.

Cameron tossed his spectacles down on the desk and rose eagerly to meet her. 'Och, we'll have to be quick, you filthy mistress. I have somewhere I have to go soon,' he said, reaching for her. 'Where shall we do it?'

Grabbing his tie, she walked backward out of the office, drawing him with her. 'I want to do it on her chair again. It makes me smile whenever I think of her sitting there after we've made love on it. The stupid cow!'

He gave a throaty laugh. 'That's just what she is. An ungrateful stupid cow of the first order. You really don't like her either, do you?'

'Why should I? The way she treats you, but she'll get her comeuppance soon, won't she?'

'I'm working on it, darling. But we have to think about your situation. About Bruce and your kids.'

She grabbed his hair and kissed him again. 'We'll think about all them later. Right now it's just about us.'

With his pipe charged and lit, Lachlan ambled over to the St Ninian's golf course, leaving a trail of tobacco smoke in his wake, where he met George Corlin-MacLeod on the first tee as they had arranged the day before.

'I haven't brought a hipflask, Padre,' said the distillery owner, opening his bag and taking out one of the Glen Corlin's distinctive handbell shaped bottle, 'but here's one of our 50-year-old Glen Corlins that I'd like you to have.'

Lachlan whistled as he took the bottle. 'There is no need for this at all, George. I am more than happy to have a few holes and a chat about your worries. Life often throws these things at us and as I always say, a problem shared is a problem halved.' He raised his bushy eyebrows questioningly. 'And maybe have a prayer afterwards, like yesterday?'

George reached into a pocket and drew out a new ball and a fresh tee. 'Well, I can't turn that down. It helped me and I'm grateful to you for letting me use you as a sounding board.' His lips tightened and he shook his head. 'After what happened to those poor kids I'd say we all have a lot to pray about. Shall I drive off first?'

'Ready golf, George. Away we go.'

They had elected to play a full eighteen holes, going round the St Ninian's course three times. As they reached the last tee, George surprised Lachlan.

'If you don't mind, Padre, I think I'd like to break open that bottle.'

'A stirrup cup before the last hole? That's not a bad idea, but let me give you a drink from my hipflask, if it won't offend you?'

George looked at him quizzically. 'Why would I be offended, Padre?'

'Because I have it filled with Abhainn Dhonn, your competitor's whisky.'

George gave a wry smile. 'Actually, I wouldn't care if it was just peatreek. I could do with a dram.'

Lachlan produced his pewter hipflask and two small leather covered whisky cups from a pocket of his bag and handed the cups to George. 'You will find it a good drop and with quite a distinctive nose,' he said as he poured a generous measure into each vessel.

The distillery owner sniffed his drink and nodded his approval before raising the cup to Lachlan. 'Here's to the last hole, Padre. I appreciate you giving me all this time in spite of all that's going on here on West Uist, with those teenagers and everything.'

'*Slainte mhath*,' Lachlan said, raising his own cup and taking a sip. 'That's not a problem, George. I am here for you if you want to talk. I deliberately didn't mention anything about this unfortunate business since I realise that you have things on your mind.'

'The golf has helped to calm my mind, but you may have noticed that over the last few holes I've been a bit nervy.'

'You are working up to telling me about your troubles.'

'It's awkward, Padre.'

'You said that the last time.'

'It's a sexual matter.'

Lachlan looked around to ensure that there was no-one within earshot. 'Would you like to go into the church where it is private to tell me?'

George shook his head and drained his whisky. 'No, we should finish the game. My problem is that I have trouble in the bedroom department, Padre.'

Lachlan was taken aback. 'In that case, George, I am not really qualified to help you. It's a doctor that you are perhaps needing to see, not a minister.'

'No need. You see, I know exactly why I have the problem. It's entirely psychological.'

'But George, I'm just a man of the cloth. I'm not a psychologist. If it is anxiety that you think is causing your problem, then a professional might —'

George handed the cup back. 'I'm not anxious, Padre. I'm angry. Bloody angry! I want to kill someone and I'm scared that I might just do it. That's why I need help.' And then, almost nonchalantly he teed up his ball. 'Shall we finish the round before the mist closes in again?'

Vicky had no idea what time it was. Deprived of any sensory input apart from her hearing, she had found herself drifting in and out of sleep. There in the bleak darkness of her mind grotesque dream images would jolt her back to her current nightmarish reality.

Her headache had lessened in intensity so that the pounding had turned into a constant background aching. The nausea had persisted, but had been gradually diminished by two other unpleasant sensations. First was an intense thirst such as she had never experienced in her life and second was the increasing pressure as her bladder started to fill up. Her mind latched onto both to increase her discomfort and state of fear.

She thought she heard a slight scratching noise, like a door being slowly pushed closed. She wanted to cry out and demand if there was anyone there, but the tape was too tight and she could not open her mouth.

Suddenly, her hair was grabbed and her head roughly yanked back so that her face was pointing up to goodness only knew where. She felt her heart pounding fast and could feel a violent pulsation in her abdomen as blood pumped through her aorta.

She felt a pressure on her mouth and heard a slight ripping noise as if the tape was being cut. Then the hand holding her hair tightened and pulled her head further back and something was thrust through a hole in the tape, forcing itself through her lips and between her teeth into her mouth. A tube of some sort.

Panic set in and she felt her breathing quicken.

There was no sound, no voice. No spark of kindness.

Water began to trickle slowly into her parched mouth and she eagerly swallowed, feeling some relief from the awful thirst. She had no idea how much water she was given before the flow stopped. When it began again she was horrified at the raw, burning taste. It was whisky. She desperately tried to blow it back, but the attempt made her gag as the end of the tube was shoved further back in her mouth, almost down her throat.

Panic stricken, she swallowed and swallowed until the flow stopped for a few seconds before water again was trickled into her mouth. Then the tube was pulled free and her head released.

She tried to mumble the word why, but only a guttural noise came out. Another long ripping noise was followed by pressure on her mouth and then she knew only too clearly that more tape was being wound round her face, plugging the hole.

Her thinking became really difficult and she knew that the whisky was rapidly kicking in and making her feel sleepy.

Moments later, she heard the scratching of wood on stone again. She knew that her captor had gone.

Blind fear helped in her struggle to stay awake and try to think. There hadn't been time to dole out the same treatment to Catriona and Jamie, which meant only one thing.

I'm all alone!

CHAPTER NINE

Torquil was riding the Bullet when his phone went off in his pocket. He immediately slowed down, coasted into a layby and switched off the engine. He slipped his goggles up and answered. It was Lorna calling him from Stornoway about the post-mortem.

'Are you all right, darling? Was it awful?'

'It was really horrible, Torquil, seeing a young lad like that being cut open.'

'Who performed the post-mortem?'

There was a pause as she consulted her notes and read from them. 'A Dr Giles Lamont. He's a forensic pathologist with the Crown Office and Procurator Fiscal's office in Oban. He came over and did the post-mortem in the hospital PM room.'

'What was his verdict?'

'Well, you know the score, he was emphatic that the post-mortem is just the start of the process.'

'So it was inconclusive?'

'No, far from it. Young Jamie had a kidney trouble, which may have contributed to his death. He showed me. His left kidney was healthy looking, but the right one was tiny and hadn't developed. Dr Lamont thinks it may never have been a functioning organ. He diagnosed it as renal dysplasia. He said it is not that uncommon and that because the left one worked, he would never have had any symptoms.'

'So how does that contribute to his death?'

'It's complicated, but it has to do with what happens to the methanol in the body. An enzyme called alcohol dehydrogenase in the liver breaks all types of alcohol down.

Ethanol, that's ordinary alcohol, gets broken down into relatively harmless compounds. Methanol though, gets broken down into formaldehyde. That gets broken down by another enzyme called aldehyde dehydrogenase into formic acid. That is nasty toxic stuff that poisons the liver, the kidneys and the nervous system.'

'And that was a problem because he only had one working kidney?'

'That's right. The formic acid is removed from the body by the kidneys and it would have been poisoned by the formic acid. That would have caused a vicious cycle because the formic acid would mount up very quickly and affect his brain and nervous system. Dr Lamont said he'll need to have blood, stomach contents, urine and other body fluids tested for methanol, formaldehyde and especially the formic acid.'

'It's as well that Ralph McLelland took bloods when he confirmed death. So was the respiratory paralysis the cause of death?'

'It's complicated, so bear with me. He was pretty sure it was asphyxiation, but there are two possible reasons for that. It looks like he had what they call a pulmonary aspiration, which means he had inhaled vomit. There was vomit in his lungs and in his trachea, probably enough to cut off his airway. That means he may have choked on his vomit. Death can occur very quickly when that happens. His brain had little haemorrhages that he called petechiae and his lungs were also covered in them, which he said is suggestive of asphyxiation. So, poor Jamie either stopped breathing and had a fit as a result of the respiratory paralysis or he inhaled vomit and choked, causing him to have a fit.'

Torquil clicked his tongue. 'I see, complicated indeed. But one way or another the methyl alcohol is the indirect cause of death.'

'That's right. As I say, we'll know more after all the lab work and the microscopy has been done.'

Torquil sighed as he took out his notebook and pen and jotted down all the salient points. 'Send me a copy of all this will you, darling. It will help until we get the full report.'

'OK. I'll email them across in a few minutes. Where are you?'

'I'm by the roadside. I was on the Bullet, but I'll be going straight to the station now and I'll get it then. So, did you have a chance to visit Catriona McDonald?'

'I did, and I talked to both the consultant nephrologist and the ophthalmologist. It's early days, but she should recover her vision. Catriona's mother was with her when I saw her. The poor kid feels grotty and she's understandably really emotional, as is her mother. Catriona just can't remember much at all. She's devastated about Jamie and upset that Vicky has not turned up yet.'

'Was it just a post exam adventure?'

'It was. Apparently Vicky and Catriona had told wee porkies about where they were. She said that Jamie just does what he wants anyway. Jamie had brought the peatreek bottle and Vicky and she had brought the cola and the nibbles. She thinks they all just got drunk and passed out. In the morning she woke up, couldn't see anything and stumbled outside. That was when Morag found her, I think.'

She paused, then: 'Any news about Vicky?'

'Nothing yet, but I'm expecting Morag to call soon.'

'Well, like they say about no news.'

After Lorna called off, Torquil sat drumming his fingers on the tank of the Bullet. He was worried and seriously doubted the wisdom of the old axiom. In this case, no news certainly didn't seem like good news.

Nathan Westwood was busy painting in the studio at the back of his Art and Antique Gallery when the door opened and Helen Beamish came in.

'Nathan, I've come about that commission,' she called through, more to make sure that there was no-one in the studio with him.

A curtain swished and he appeared, wiping a brush with a cloth. 'Ah yes, I'm interested in that, Mrs Beamish.' Then lowering his voice. 'Would you like to come through to my studio to discuss it?'

As she walked past him he crossed to the door and glanced through the window at the misty street to make sure no one was approaching the gallery from either direction. He clicked the latch on the door and turned the sign round to read 'Closed.'

Once behind the curtain, Helen flung her arms about his neck and kissed him passionately. 'God, I've missed you,' she said, finally, breaking their clinch.

Nathan nodded in the direction of the chaise longue that he used to make sketches or photograph clients, and which he and Helen used on occasions for urgent or opportunist sex.

She shook her head regretfully. 'There isn't time, darling. We have to be so careful now and can't afford any more stupid mistakes. We've both got too much to lose.'

Nathan scowled. 'Does he suspect?'

'He suspects something. He's been watching me closely and I think he's been following me. I found some high powered binoculars in the garage. They're new. He lied to me and said he'd come back early because the case had been settled already.

Well, I checked and it had, but the day before. I think he came back to the island the night before to spy on me. To spy on us!'

'Christ! Then we might need to think about —'

She put a finger to his lips. 'We have to be extra careful and make sure we cover our tracks.'

Ewan had spent the past hour on the phone dealing with islanders worried about Vicky or wanting news about Catriona. He gave them all as much information as he was able to, always maintaining his usual polite manner.

Penny's door was ajar and she had found herself listening with more than half an ear. Try as she might to just get on with her own work she realised how much she liked his lilting accent and his ever friendly manner. She felt guilty about being so clinical earlier, so she went out.

'Would you — er — like a cup of tea, Ewan?' she asked, standing with her hands in her pockets. 'I'd better get used to making it, since I'm the new kid on the block, so to speak.'

Ewan beamed at her. 'Oh, that would be grand, Penny. Shall I show you where everything is?'

She toed the floor and immediately wanted to rebuke herself. *Stop behaving like a sixteen-year-old. Just make him a cup of tea and then get back to work.*

The bell rang and the outer door opened. A moment later Calum Steele came in.

'Ah, Constable McPhee, the very man I wanted to see,' he said in a deliberately sing-song manner. He grinned and then seeing Penny behind Ewan, he became serious. 'You will be the new Detective Constable, I think?' he said, stepping right up to the counter and extending a hand across it.

'DC Penny Faversham,' Ewan introduced, 'meet Calum Steele, the editor of the *West Uist Chronicle*. He sniffs out the news like no one else.'

Calum stood straight and puffed out his chest. 'Oh, we journalists have our ways of picking up information.'

'Pleased to meet you, Calum,' Penny replied, shaking his hand. 'And how exactly did you learn about me?'

Calum tapped the side of his nose. 'Sorry, it is a golden rule of journalism, DC Faversham, we never reveal our sources,' he said in his most practised enigmatic manner. Then with a click of his tongue: 'You've arrived on the island in the middle of a tragic happening, of course. I just popped in to see how Angus Mackintosh is bearing up. Is there any news on Vicky Spiers?'

'Inspector McKinnon took him to see the body and he's understandably distraught. He insisted on going home. As for Vicky, I have no new information, Calum,' Ewan replied.

'Pity. And what about Robbie Ochterlonie? That was a sad case.' He motioned as if he was about to drink from an invisible glass. 'Too much whisky, I hear?'

Penny had been warned about Calum by Lorna and understood that he was fishing for information. 'I'm afraid that we are not in a position to comment yet, Calum. It is an unexpected death and has been referred to the Procurator Fiscal, so we are awaiting the result of the post-mortem examination.'

'Ah, that's what I thought. Is Torquil in yet?'

Ewan assured him that he wasn't.

'Well, tell him if he wants any more help from the *Chronicle* to give me a bell.' He nodded to them. 'Good to meet you, Penny. I look forward to working with you and getting to know you better.'

Once the newspaperman had gone Ewan gave a short laugh. 'That's typical of Calum Steele. He came in just to check you out, you know. If you hadn't been in the office he'd have had some ploy to get introduced to you. He can be a nuisance, but he's basically a good lad.'

'Well, now he knows about me, why don't we take this opportunity while it's quiet to do the same. The boss gave me some tasks to do and I've got a five minutes to spare, so how about if I make that tea and you can explain to me about this highland hammer and those murder shoes of yours.'

When Torquil arrived at the station he told Ewan and Penny that he wanted to have a meeting with the team in half an hour.

'What about the search — will Morag be coming back?' Ewan asked.

'No, they've found a trainer in mud near the old Strathshiffin Road. There's a good chance it's one of Vicky's, so we'll need to check. Morag will be moving the search area accordingly. I'm bringing the twins in and we'll skype Morag.'

Once the Drummond twins arrived back, both dressed in their heavy waterproofs rather than police uniforms, Ewan came in with a tray of mugs of tea.

'Things have moved on, folks,' Torquil said, sitting behind his desk and referring to his notebook. 'Firstly, Lorna called me to say she attended the post-mortem on Jamie Mackintosh. The pathologist has to look at slides and get the results of tests back, but he was convinced that he had only one working kidney, which meant he wasn't able to clear the methanol and all the toxins from his body. He either vomited and inhaled his vomit, or he choked and then had a fit. Essentially, whatever the prime mechanism, he asphyxiated.'

Penny winced. 'That's horrible. He drowned in his own vomit.'

Torquil nodded. 'And if the bottle from the pillbox is shown to have contained methyl alcohol then whoever supplied it could be facing a charge of culpable homicide.'

Penny whistled and opened the file in her hands. 'In that case it really is serious, boss. I checked with Ian Gillesbie, the Senior Scene Examiner and the first results are back. The bottle had an extremely high concentration of methanol in it.' She ran a finger down the page. 'They also tested the blood samples that Dr McLelland took and they'll be testing samples that the pathologist takes straight from the body. They'll be able to see if it matches, although it sounds as if there isn't much doubt.'

Wallace was sitting with his arms folded. 'So this was definitely peatreek?'

'Looks like it,' said Torquil.

'How did they get hold of it?' Douglas asked.

'Catriona McDonald told Lorna that Jamie brought it.'

'And where did he get it from?' Ewan asked. 'Does Angus have a still?'

'That's what we need to find out, Ewan,' Torquil replied. 'There must be several home stills around the island.'

He turned to Penny. 'Illicit distilling used to be common on the islands. Folk had them on farms, on crofts or on one of the many isles around the coast. We need to find them all and have their whisky confiscated and checked for methanol.'

'Shall I do that, boss?' Penny asked.

'No, Wallace and Douglas can do that. They know the island and they probably have a good idea of who could be distilling.'

Wallace harrumphed. 'It may be not so simple, Piper. These days all sorts of folk are distilling spirits. Rum, gin, vodka. You can get the tackle on the internet, no bother.'

Torquil nodded, recollecting only too well his conversation with Lorna about whisky for their wedding favours. 'Aye, Lorna was talking about this. Artisan gin, she called it. She even knows where to get it on the island. I'll need to find out from her.' He turned again to Penny. 'What I need you to do is find out everything about whisky making, especially illicit whisky and how they make peatreek. Also, delve into the medical details. We need to know all about methanol, its properties, toxic amounts, the works.'

Douglas had been sipping his tea and held the mug up reflectively. 'This is a really strong cup of tea.'

Ewan beamed. 'Aye, just the way everyone likes it.'

Douglas tapped the mug with a fingernail. 'That's as maybe, but I was thinking that the strength is something that can vary, just as the strength of peatreek must vary. There won't be any quality control over it.'

Wallace nodded. 'Aye, but that's just the strength of the alcohol. There shouldn't be any methyl alcohol in it at all.'

'That's exactly right,' said Torquil. 'That's the point about distilling. The first alcohol to come out of the distillation process is the methanol, because it has a lower boiling point. They call that the foreshot and they throw it away. Penny, I want you to visit the newest proper distillery, it's owned by Hamish McNab. That's a good place to familiarise yourself with the process after you've done a bit of research. Speak to Hamish McNab and also have a word with Keith Finlay, his head distiller. Hamish poached him from the Glen Corlin distillery a few years ago. He's a decent chap and he'll explain the whole process. We need to know what they do with their foreshot. I'll be doing the same at the Glen Corlin distillery.'

'I'm just a bit worried, Piper,' Wallace stated. 'There may be a good chance that whoever supplied this peatreek has disposed of their still and of their peatreek.'

'That's why we need to move fast and also why we need to keep quiet about this. That means being careful about what we tell the media.'

Ewan snapped his fingers. 'Calum Steele was in earlier. He came to check out DC Faversham, I think, but he was doing his usual fishing. He asked for you to call him when you have more information, boss.'

Penny nodded. 'He was also asking about the other death. I told him we were waiting on the post-mortem.'

'I'll deal with Calum,' Torquil replied. He sat forward and touched the mouse on his desk to open his computer. 'Right, now about Vicky Spiers. Let's skype Morag.'

The others clustered round behind Torquil as Morag's image appeared on the screen. They could see the shelves of books behind her as she sat at the small desk inside the library van.

'We've moved the base to the Strathshiffin Road layby,' she informed them. 'Douglas has the trainer all bagged up.'

'It's on the desk in front of me, Morag,' said Torquil. 'It's an Adidas trainer and looks fairly new. We'll be checking if it's Vicky's with the Spiers straight after this. Any fresh developments?'

'Nothing new. But the teams are scouring the area inch by inch. I've lost a lot, though. I have only a third of the folk that I had yesterday.'

'Well, we can't make people volunteer. We just have to be grateful for those who give their time.' He quickly gave her a recap on the result of the post-mortem. 'So it's a possible culpable homicide case now. We're going to begin searching for illicit stills on the island and also check the two distilleries for how they deal with their foreshot. Do you have any idea of anyone who's making their own whisky or other spirits?'

'There is Maisie McIvor on Harbour Street. She makes artisan gin. It's not an illicit still, though. She has a rectifier's licence as it's all small scale. Lorna and I were talking about wedding favours only the other day.'

Torquil grimaced as he recalled the phone conversation he had with Lorna. He had not realised that Morag and she had already been talking about it. He forced himself to keep his mind on the important matter in hand and not be diverted. There would be plenty of time to think about the wedding later.

'Aye, Lachlan also mentioned her to me. He said she makes fragrances. But how about anyone else?'

Morag shook her head. 'I don't know, I'm afraid. Is there anything else you want me to do?'

'No, you've got your hands full there. Leave the trainer with us to identify and just let us know if anything else turns up. Hopefully it will be when we find Vicky alive and well.'

Penny had gone out of the office to answer her phone during the skype session. She came back in eager to tell the others her news.

'That was Ian Gillesbie,' she said. 'More results. Firstly, the fingerprinting at the pillbox only showed up three sets of prints. It looks likely that they were only from the teenagers.'

'And the second thing?' asked Torquil.

'They tested the bottle of whisky residue from Robbie Ochterlonie's cabin. It is exactly the same composition as the stuff in the bottle from the pillbox!'

Torquil sat back in his chair and blew air through his lips. 'That's no coincidence, then, is it? They must be from the same source.' He drummed his fingers on his desk. 'And Vicky Spiers worked part time at the Hydro along with Catriona McDonald. Task number one is to see if the trainer is Vicky's. Then the second task is to find out exactly where these bottles of peatreek came from.' He allocated tasks to them. 'OK people, let's get started.'

CHAPTER TEN

The Spiers lived in a prefabricated bungalow on Kincardine Terrace at the top of Kyleshiffin. It had a fine view of the harbour and had been converted with ramps and widened doors for Brock Spiers' wheelchair.

Mist was still hanging over the town as Torquil walked to their house after the meeting at the station. He was met at the door by Jeannie Spiers. A small, pretty woman in her late forties, her face was haggard.

'What news, Inspector McKinnon?' she asked as she held the door open for him. 'Just go through, Brock is in the living room. He's — having a drink.'

Torquil gathered her meaning and went in ahead to find Brock Spiers by the window staring out over the harbour, a large glass of whisky in his hand.

'Good morning, Brock. I'm afraid that we still haven't found Vicky, but we —'

'Then what the hell are you doing here?' Brock snapped in a slurred voice. He turned his self-propelled wheelchair and moved it forward over the linoleum to within a couple of feet of Torquil. 'Our daughter has been missing since Sunday night and you lot have done nothing.'

'We've got search parties out at this moment, Brock. We've got an army of volunteers — your neighbours, friends and old workmates. They are all —'

'Workmates?' Brock repeated belligerently. 'That's right! Remind me that I'm not able to be out there myself, but my old workmates are.' He took a hefty swig of his whisky. 'Damn few of my workmates ever come near this place, you know.

Scared, I reckon, in case their boss the spider woman thinks I'll get at them.'

'Brock, please. This isn't the time,' Jeannie remonstrated.

'After seven years you'd think that some of them could be counted as friends. Well, no way. Oh, I have a couple of good pals still, but they are also considered deserters from the high and mighty Glen Corlins. Keith Finlay and Jerry McColl both work for Hamish McNab now. They come, they have a drink with me. They care!'

'We care about Vicky, Brock,' Torquil said.

'You care, they care! We had that slip of a lass, Cora Melville from the *Chronicle*. As nice as ninepence, sympathetic and all that, but we know she just wants a story. What do you expect when she works with that Calum Steele.'

'Brock!' Jeannie persisted. 'Inspector McKinnon is here about Vicky so just hold your tongue and let him speak, will you.'

Torquil held up the briefcase he was carrying. 'We've found a trainer and we need to know if it is Vicky's. We think she may have been stumbling around and it got stuck in the mud. If we can establish that it is hers then we'll know that we are in a better place to search from.'

'Let's see it then, please,' said Jeannie, sitting on the settee pushed up against the wall so that Brock had maximum room to manoeuvre his wheelchair.

Torquil opened the case and took out the trainer, still in the polythene specimen bag.

Jeannie's reaction told Torquil what he suspected. She clapped both hands to her mouth and suppressed a shriek. Tears welled up in her eyes and she nodded her head emphatically.

'It's Vicky's right enough,' said Brock, sounding more sober. 'Please find her for us, Inspector McKinnon.'

After leaving the Spiers' house Torquil walked to the *West Uist Chronicle* offices, and was pleased to see Calum's yellow Lambretta was parked against the kerb. Torquil pushed open the door and triggered the bell in the office above. Taking the steps three at a time he bounded up and found both Calum and Cora hard at work on their computers.

Cora, always full of verve rose instantly to greet him, while Calum wheeled round in his swivel chair and leaned back.

'Welcome to the press room, Piper,' Calum said, picking up a pencil and tapping his desk with it. 'Any fresh leads?'

'As a matter of fact that's why I'm here.'

'Has the post-mortem on Jamie Mackintosh been done?'

Torquil had worked out how he was going to play it with Calum. 'We are waiting for the official report. It should not be long. But we found this.' He opened his briefcase and took out the polythene bag containing the mud-covered trainer. 'I've just been round to see Brock and Jeannie Spiers and they confirmed it belongs to Vicky.'

Cora bent down to look at the trainer. 'I went to see them earlier. They are totally cut up. The poor man was drinking whisky this morning. I could see that his wife was worried for him as well as for their daughter.'

'We're all getting worried, Cora,' said Torquil.

'And I can tell that you're worried what we're going to write,' said Calum. 'Well, don't worry, the *West Uist Chronicle* is here to help not hinder.'

'Exactly the spirit I was hoping for, Calum. Can you take a photograph and get it out there? Ask if anyone has seen the other one?'

'Leave it with us, Piper. We'll put it on the blog and we'll send out one of our digital bulletins. We'll get it across the island as quick as you can say Jack Flash.'

'You are a couple of stars,' Torquil said as he set the bag on the table for them to photograph.

From the *Chronicle* offices Torquil went back to the station, picked up the Bullet and rode up to the Old Hydro Residential Home. Doreen McGuire greeted him at the door and asked him a barrage of questions about the terrible situation as she led the way along the corridor to the manager's office where Norma Ferguson was sitting behind the desk making out worksheets. Torquil could see from the patina of perspiration on her brow that she was feeling stressed.

He refused the offer of tea and before she too hit him with the same questions he took the initiative and told her about the finding of the trainer, now identified as belonging to Vicky Spiers.

'So I need to know more about how Vicky settled in here.'

Norma leaned forward and clasped her hands in front of her on the desk. 'She's one of three part time girls who are all studying at the Academy, doing their Highers year. She and Catriona McDonald have been with us all this year.' Tears welled up in her eyes. 'Oh, Inspector McKinnon, this is so dreadful and what with finding Robbie dead like that.'

'I understand, Norma. It must have been a dreadful shock.'

'I'll never forget it as long as I live.'

'Did you touch anything when you went in?'

'No, I told DC Faversham I just checked his pulse to see if he was alive. I knew he was dead. He was just like some of our residents when they pass away overnight and we find them in the morning. That's a nice way to go I always think, but poor Robbie, that was horrible. No-one should die alone like that.'

'Have you been in touch with Catriona or Vicky's parents?'

'Oh yes, it was one of the first things I did after I heard about what happened at the old pillbox. I went round to see them, actually. I thought it was the least that I could do. It … it's what Robbie would have done.'

Unable to hold back the tears any longer she began to sob. Torquil reached over the desk and patted her hand.

'Let it out, Norma. It's natural that you'll feel upset.'

'I … I just feel so helpless. I don't think I could have done anything to stop what happened to the girls and poor Jamie Mackintosh, but I can't help thinking that I should have been able to help Robbie. I'm just so gullible and believed him when he told me he wanted to be a writer.' She pulled out a paper handkerchief from the box on the desk and blew her nose. Then: 'I think I loved him, Inspector. I think he liked me too, but neither of us have ever said anything. Maybe he'd still be alive if —'

'Norma, there is no point in letting your mind do that to yourself. You have nothing to feel guilty about. But tell me, what did he write? I wasn't aware that Robbie was a writer.'

She gave a brief smile. 'I think it was wishful thinking, really. He always had a laptop with him and was forever tapping away at it in spare moments. He talked about his novel and how it was going, but none of us know anything more than that. He had a cheeky way of putting us off and said that one day we'd be able to read it, when he was on his way to being rich and famous.'

'You said you were gullible, do you think he wasn't telling the truth?'

'It was Millie McKendrick, one of the older care assistants who told me. She'd known him for a lot longer than me. She used to roll her eyes when he went on about his writing, especially if he was going to spend his weekend off in his writing cabin. Then one day she told me he built the cabin not to write, but to drink his peatreek.'

'Tell me about that, did he make his own spirits?'

Norma shook her head. 'I don't know, Inspector. You'd maybe be better asking Millie herself.'

Torquil nodded. 'I will. But now about Catriona, she seems to be doing better in the hospital. Her vision is clearing, so I hear. Her mother is staying at the hospital with her. Catriona told Sergeant Golspie that Jamie Mackintosh brought the bottle of peatreek that they were drinking. Where do you think he got it?'

'I don't know that either, Inspector. I saw Jamie now and then, he was friends with the two girls, but he didn't work here or have any connection with the Hydro.'

Torquil lifted his briefcase and opened it to show her the bag containing Vicky's trainer. 'Do you recognise this?'

'Adidas! That's Vicky's right enough. She liked her trainers and she liked her shoes. She was always saying that she was saving up to buy some Alexander McQueen trainers or a pair of Jimmy Choo shoes. She liked her high heels almost as much as her trainers, you see. She and Catriona were quite similar that way and were always talking about what they would be wearing when they went to uni.'

'What did they say about uni?'

'Catriona is planning to go into nursing and Vicky was planning to do something with people, though maybe not caring specifically. She was talking about studying to be a dental hygienist. She had been looking at the University of Dundee or the University of the Highlands and Islands.'

He put the trainer away. 'Norma, you've been very helpful. Now if you don't mind I'd like to have a chat with Millie.'

'Of course, she'll be on the west wing doing the tea round, so I'll give her a buzz and I'll take over from her. You can stay here and use the office.'

Millie McKendrick had worked at the Old Hydropathic Residential Home for twenty-two years and was devoted to her job. She was about five foot two in height, fairly slim, but with forearms that were well developed from all her years of lifting residents. Torquil knew her as a stalwart of the church, ever ready to help out at St Ninian events. He also knew from his uncle that although she was not exactly teetotal she had strong views about alcohol.

After adroitly fielding her questions he asked her about Robbie Ochterlonie's writing and his writing cabin.

Millie laughed. 'Don't tell me that Norma still has the impression that Robbie is any kind of a writer? I'm heartbroken that he's dead, but he certainly never did any writing in that cabin. Oh, he was always on his laptop pretending to write, but he was a fantasist, was our Robbie. He liked to drink that filthy peatreek, which was stupid for him and his diabetes. Me and Doreen McGuire were always telling him to be careful with it. But oh no, he'd go to his place at Lochiel's Copse and drink himself stupid. Not only that, but he supplied some of the residents with the stuff, the idiot. If the owners had ever found out he'd have been out on his ear.'

'Norma Ferguson seems to have had a soft spot for him?'

'Aye, well, Robbie was probably not the right sort for her. He was secretive, as you may have gathered. I think he was a bit duplicitous, too.'

'What makes you say that, Millie?'

The care assistant scrunched her nose up. 'I don't know exactly, it's just that he would have times when he was always making secret phone calls, shutting himself away in his office to do it. Like he was having an affair.'

'So he was a ladies' man?'

'Not exactly. Oh, Norma had a candle for him, but he was no oil painting and he didn't really put himself about, if you know what I mean. Not publicly. I'm sure Doreen and me would have known if he had a relationship on the island.'

'Could he have been having an affair with a married woman? Or could he have been gay?'

Millie shrugged her shoulders. 'I don't think he was gay. I just think he might have been having a relationship he wanted to keep secret.'

'You've no evidence though, have you, Millie? Is it just a suspicion?'

'Aye, it's a hunch. But my hunches are usually good.'

Torquil hummed and leaned forward and made a few notes in his book, then said, 'So where did he get his peatreek, Millie? Did he have a still somewhere? Was that why he buried himself away in Lochiel's Copse?'

'That I don't know and I don't really want to know. I don't like drink and I don't like what it does to people. All that's been happening lately must surely get the message through to people. It's all just poison.'

Her mouth had been getting tighter as she spoke until it was now just a disapproving line. 'Don't misunderstand me, Inspector. I'm going to miss him, but I can't help feeling he brought things on his own head. Ask Doreen McGuire, she might know more.'

Five minutes later Torquil was looking across the desk at Doreen McGuire. While Millie was on the petite end of the spectrum, Doreen was large and curvaceous. Like Millie she was a stalwart of the church and of the Mother's Union.

'Millie tells me that she thinks Robbie might have been having a secret relationship. Could that be true?'

Doreen shrugged. 'I think she could be right.'

'Any reason to suppose that?'

'Robbie used to joke a lot. Banter, flirtatious stuff, you know. Never with any of the youngsters, just with me and Millie. You probably know that Millie likes to pretend that she's a prude, but she has a naughty side to her. She likes the banter, too. We think he just did it with us because we were safe, he would know that was as far as it went. But sometimes his banter changed. Less of the innuendo and flirty behaviour to more of the "guess what I've been up to" sort of talk. But he would never elaborate. It was conspiratorial chatter, but he'd end it with a look that said "wouldn't you like to know?" I would say he'd been like that for the last three months or so.'

Torquil jotted some of the things she said verbatim into his notebook.

'But why would that matter, Inspector? Robbie was entitled to his private life, wasn't he?'

'Of course he was, except if he was seeing someone who could have been supplying him with peatreek. Especially if it was poisonous peatreek.'

Doreen gasped. 'And you think it could be the same stuff as the youngsters had been drinking?'

'We have to consider all possibilities, Doreen. Millie said that Robbie drank himself silly with peatreek at his cabin and that he also supplied some of the residents with it.'

'Oh dear, Millie and I often thought he'd get in trouble over that. I think he was just being nice to them. Giving them wee bottles so they could have a dram in their rooms when they wanted. And peatreek would just seem a bit naughty, so it would give them a bit of excitement in their lives.'

'I need to know which residents he supplied, Doreen. I need to make sure that they haven't got dangerous peatreek in their possession that could make them ill.'

Doreen looked worried. 'Could we do this with Norma present? I don't want her to think we've by-passed her.'

'Of course. And once we have their names I'll need to confiscate any peatreek in their possession and have it analysed.'

'Oh Lord, we don't want any of our residents getting poisoned.'

'Just one more thing before we get Norma. Do you know if Robbie had access to a still himself?'

Doreen shook her head.

'Any idea who supplied him?'

'Absolutely no idea.'

Doreen led Torquil over to a group of the Hydro's residents, who she suspected may have accepted whisky from Robbie. The group was headed by eighty-six-year-old Stuart Robertson. A retired trawler captain and ex-publican, he was used to being in charge, and he essentially dominated his little coterie of fellow residents, enjoying the company of a favoured trio who never failed to be amused by his anecdotes and tales of derring-do upon the sea. Husband and wife, Murdoch and

Agnes Shand, both also lively octogenarians and Norman Kirk a seventy-seven-year-old former gamekeeper from Islay all joined Stuart's protests when Torquil confronted them in their corner of the snug, the room where they sat round what they called 'the Captain's Table' playing interminable games of whist, brag or poker.

'Will we get our bottles back after they've been tested, Inspector?' Stuart asked. 'We pay Robbie good money for that, you know.'

'I'm afraid not. It's to be confiscated,' Torquil replied. 'I'll give you a receipt, but that's all.'

'Are we in trouble, Inspector McKinnon?' Agnes asked. 'We don't have much of it, just a wee tot at night and maybe a teaspoon in a cup of tea when it's chilly.' She shook her head. 'It's a terrible thing that happened to those teenagers.'

'Terrible,' her husband agreed. 'A waste of life.'

'Maybe we'll find out where Robbie got the stuff from,' said Norman. 'He was always one for keeping secrets, that was our Robbie.'

Stuart Robertson was used to having the last word. 'Aye, he liked his secrets right enough. He was always saying, "a word to the wise". Never a truer thing spoken.'

He began to laugh and the other three residents followed suit. They were still laughing as Norma came with a bag of bottles that she had retrieved from their rooms.

Millie McKendrick was passing behind her and heard the clinking of bottles. 'I knew you lot would get into trouble over that drinking.'

Angus Mackintosh was feeling emotionally numb. His leg hurt like hell, despite the painkillers, and he was limping with the heavily bandaged leg.

He had made a vow with himself never to drink again. The realisation that his son had died in that miserable Second World War pillbox had sent his mind into overdrive. He had not been as low since his wife had died after having a subarachnoid haemorrhage three years before.

I let him down again, he thought. *I wasn't there for him, just like I haven't been there for him ever since his mother died. I crept into a bottle and he grew up himself. He did all sorts of little jobs for folk on the island and I just let him do it. I didn't take near enough interest in him and I guess he resented me for it.*

He dissolved in tears for the umpteenth time and sat with his head in his hands. It was only when the sobbing subsided and he looked up and surveyed the wrecked sitting room of his cottage that any semblance of forward action presented itself to him.

Someone's going to pay for this. I'm not having Jamie dying for nothing. He had a future that has just been rubbed out.

He got up and went through to Jamie's room.

It's a midden, right enough. I'll need to tidy it up soon, once the hurting reduces.

He picked up a discarded t-shirt, one of Jamie's favourite's, and held it to his nose. It smelled of Jamie and triggered another bout of sobbing as he buried his face in it.

Out of the corner of his eye he spied the pile of American comics beside the bed, next to a couple of ring binder files with his work for his Highers. What did McKinnon say he thought had happened? They had been celebrating and had been drinking peatreek and lemonade or stuff.

He limped over to the comics and knelt by the bed. Underneath it he saw the rucksack and pulled it out. It clinked as he did so.

What have we got here, Jamie. More of this peatreek?

But it wasn't. It was an assortment of stuff, a bottle of lemonade, a new wristwatch, umpteen chocolate bars, some brand new unread paperbacks, packets of cigarettes and a couple of pouches of hand-rolling tobacco. Lastly, a box of condoms.

You were up to your old tricks, weren't you, Jamie? Pinching things. And it looks like you were hoping to start some new tricks. Sex, is that what you were doing up at the pillbox with those two girls? Where did you get the peatreek that McKinnon said you had drunk?

He hefted the bottle in his hand and cursed as anger welled up inside him.

I'm going to find who you got it from and then I'm going to pour poison down their bloody throat.

As he stood up he noticed the diary on the shelf under the bedside table. He picked it up and ran his hand over the cover before opening it to read his son's characteristic handwriting. He knew that Jamie had always kept a diary, but he had never thought to look inside. It would have been like spying on his thoughts. But now he wanted to know what he had been thinking. What he had been doing these last few years while he had been growing up, sharing the same house, but not really sharing anything important. And now it was too late.

His grip on the diary tightened and his eyes widened as he read.

The latest *West Uist Chronicle* email issue arrived in a multitude of inboxes all over the island.

The headline suddenly appeared: **VICKY'S TRAINER FOUND**

Bridget McDonald read the email as she sat by her daughter's bedside. It had been a relief when the haemodialysis treatment was completed and the blood tests showed that Catriona's life was no longer considered in danger, although the consultant nephrologist had told them that she would have to stay under observation for a few days to monitor her kidney function.

'They have found one of Vicky's trainers,' she told Catriona. 'Hopefully she'll have been sleeping it off somewhere and they'll find her soon.'

Catriona immediately burst into tears. 'Please God, don't let them find her dead!'

CHAPTER ELEVEN

Wallace and Douglas knew a number of folk who regularly drank peatreek and went seeking them out in order to find out who they were supplied by. They both anticipated that it would be a harder task than it actually proved to be, because everyone was aware of the tragedy that had befallen the three teenagers and were keen to help.

As Torquil had instructed they confiscated and labelled the bottles and emphasised to everyone that it could be dangerous to drink any that they had secreted away, especially unopened ones.

Only one of the imbibers, a crofter over on the Wee Kingdom had his own illicit still, which he used exclusively for his own consumption. The others were supplied by one of four still owners, all of whom kept them hidden on uninhabited islets that made up the West Uist archipelago. Like their customers, all of them cooperated and agreed to lead the Drummonds to them.

Boarding *The Seaspray*, the West Uist Police catamaran, which was always moored in the Kyleshiffin harbour in readiness for a daily round of the coast, they took the distillers, most of them actually part time fishermen like themselves, to inspect their stills. They recorded how many bottles they had stored and confiscated them before putting up official police tapes around the sites.

All took their treatment in good part, though some had parting pleas.

'You'll make sure I don't get into trouble, won't you lads?' said Tosh MacNeill. 'It could affect my business badly.'

'Whatever happens, don't let my dad know about this, will you, Douglas? He'd have my teeth for cufflinks.'

And while no-one actually offered a bribe, many future pints of Heather Ale were promised in the Bonnie Prince Charlie.

Much as they would have liked to help out pals neither Wallace nor Douglas felt able to make any rash promise. For all they knew some of the cargo of bottles they had on *The Seaspray* could be lethal.

After quickly researching on the internet about the basics of whisky production Penny had phoned the Abhainn Dhonn distillery and talked to Hamish McNab, who had just come back from the search. He sounded tired.

'Of course you can come across. We want to do whatever is needed to find young Vicky and get justice for poor Jamie Mackintosh.'

Penny set up her sat nav and drove across to the west of the island. The heavens opened on the way and she had to put her windscreen wipers on full and drive relatively slowly. Sheep were sheltering in nooks and crannies along the roadside and in the lashing rain it was hard to differentiate them from occasional boulders. And then, typical of the weather on the island, the rain abruptly stopped.

She smelled the distillery before she saw it. There was a definite tang, which seemed to be a melange of peat smoke, roasted barley and seaweed.

Cresting a hill she spotted it about a hundred yards inland from the sea, a converted farm steading consisting of a two-storied house with attached conservatory, a cluster of whitewashed outhouses and a small wind turbine. Smoke and steam billowed out of two stacks. Barley fields stretched out on either side of the road which led over a small bridge into a cobbled yard, which had been extended into a small car park.

On the whitewashed wall a large brown sign with black writing read:

ABHAINN DHONN DISTILLERY.
(Brown River)

Penny got out of her car and cast an eye at the babbling river that flowed under the bridge. She noted that it was clear, but had a definite russet brown appearance.

A door in the whitewashed building opened and two men came out. One was tall with ginger hair and a beard, dressed in a tweed sports jacket, corduroy trousers and well-polished brogues. The other was of average height and slighter build, with a high receding hairline. He was dressed in overalls, a large white apron and white wellingtons.

'DC Faversham, I am presuming,' Hamish McNab said, striding forward to shake her hand. 'Welcome to Abhainn Dhonn. I'm Hamish McNab and this is Keith Finlay, my head distiller.'

Penny shook both their hands, noting that Hamish McNab's expression was deadpan whereas Keith Finlay had dimpled cheeks, as if he always smiled. 'This is good of you to see me. I need a very quick lesson in making whisky and my inspector said that your distillery is the ideal place to go for information.'

Hamish waved a hand. 'No problem at all. We're all deeply concerned for Vicky Spiers and Catriona McDonald and utterly devastated at the death of young Jamie Mackintosh.' He shrugged his shoulders. 'It's not looking good though, is it? I received one of Calum Steele's *West Uist Chronicle* emails that said you've found a trainer. Let's hope that leads somewhere.

But we must do what we can to help you, so just have a good sniff of the air. That will give you an idea of what goes into our whisky. Peat, malted barley and good clean sea air.' He waved at the surrounding fields with their yellowing crop. 'We grow as much of our own barley here as we can, although as we increase production we are having to buy in more. I'm trying to buy more land, which isn't easy, so fingers crossed.'

'Before today I didn't know that whisky was made from barley,' Penny confessed.

Hamish nodded matter-of-factly. 'If you are a city type then there is no reason why you should know. But the type of barley is important, too. You see there are several different varieties. We use two types, Bere and Concerto. They are both early maturing and they have a low moisture content so they are good for malting.'

'And maybe just as important, we have the abhainn dhonn, which means the "brown river" on our doorstep,' said Keith Finlay. 'It comes down from the Corlins, through ancient peatbogs and over quartzite. We pump it into our holding tanks at the back of the distillery. There's no finer base for *uisge beatha* than that, in my humble opinion.'

Hamish McNab glanced at his watch and then pointed to the door. 'Come in and I'll give you a brief overview. I have to be somewhere else very soon, so I'll then leave you in Keith's capable hands. He's been in the whisky distilling business all his life, so he'll be able to answer all your questions.'

They entered a spartanly furnished room with walls covered in framed pictures of the original farm steading and its apparent transition over the years from sepia tint photographs of a small croft, into a thriving steading and then gradually into a distillery.

Hamish pointed to an old photograph of a man in front of the building they were in, working a scythe blade on a wheel sharpening stone. 'My family have lived here for four generations now. That's my great grandfather Hector McNab working this croft back at the end of the nineteenth century. You can see his boat in the distance. Back then folk eked out a living on the land and the sea.'

One by one he picked out other pictures of men and women, through the generations. Gradually, as the photographs became newer and in colour Penny could see the family resemblance and in particular the ginger hair.

'My father had built the place up and acquired other crofts so that we had a sizable farmstead. But when he died and I took it over I had plans, big plans, to diversify with a small distillery. It was not an easy matter, mind you. So many hoops to leap through, not to mention a very considerable investment. Over the years I have ploughed about two million pounds into this place, but its proving worth it these last few years.'

'When did you start, Mr McNab?'

'Eight years ago now. We're starting to build a reputation and the orders are coming in from all over the world for the Abhainn Dhonn peated single malt whisky.' He glanced at his watch again. 'But I'll need to go, so Keith will show you through the various processes now and answer any questions you have.'

'Oh, there is just one question before you go,' said Penny. 'What experience of whisky distilling did you have?'

For the first time the ghost of a smile crossed his lips. 'I maybe shouldn't admit it, but the family had always operated a wee still, just for the family's consumption. That was my forebears, mind you. No illicit whisky has ever been produced on this land as long as I have been in charge.'

Once he had gone Keith led Penny to the next long room in the centre of which stood a large round tub surmounted by a metal dome with various pipes attached. Beyond, was another large vessel connected to the first by a large pipe.

'The first thing you need to know, DC Faversham, is that whisky is essentially just distilled malted barley beer. The malting of the barley is done in the old barn. You see, barley is just starch, so we have to make it turn into sugar that we can ferment. We lay it all out and turn it and turn it, and then moisten it and heat it to really trick it into thinking it is spring. It then turns its starch into sugar.'

He pointed to the large tub. 'This is the very first process, which we call mashing and this is the mash tun. We put the ground grain into the tun and mix it with hot water, which turns this into a sort of cereal tea, that we call the "wort". See that big pipe? It's called an underback. The wort goes through that into the collecting vessel, that is called the washback. It's gently heated and yeast is added to make it ferment.'

Penny had started to make notes. 'Fascinating. And how long does that take?'

'It is there for precisely seventy-two hours. That is our time at Abhainn Dhonn, but other distilleries might be as quick as forty-eight or as long as one hundred and twenty. This is now beer and it can go on to be distilled. And that takes place next door.'

As they walked past the mash tun and the collecting vessel, Penny asked: 'How long have you worked here, Keith? I understand from my inspector that you used to work at the big distillery.'

At the door Keith turned with a knitted brow. 'I've been with Hamish McNab for seven years. It's a sore point with the Corlin-Macleods, because I was their head distiller. I don't think they ever forgave me.' His natural smile bounced back. 'Put it this way, they scored me off their Christmas card list and I barely get a nod from either of them when I'm out and about.'

'So Mr McNab wanted your expertise?'

Keith nodded. 'Aye, he did. And they were understandably concerned that I might be giving away their secrets.'

Penny nodded. 'Understandably.'

'But the truth is that the Glen Corlin range of whiskies are well established and the water they use has an entirely different character. They make both peated and unpeated whisky, whereas we concentrate on peated. At least for now. Later, who knows.'

'Were the Corlin-Macleods difficult to work for?'

This brought a hearty laugh. 'Goodness me, no. The truth is that they were easier than Hamish McNab. He has a short temper and to speak frankly, he's a bit of a potty-mouth. But he's good to us, all four of us. He also hired Jerry McColl who worked for them. Between Hamish and the four we work the farm, do the malting, distilling, warehousing and supplying. That's why I wanted to come here when Hamish offered me the chance, apart from the money, it is more of a challenge than the almost automatic whisky production at a larger distillery like Glen Corlin.'

He opened the door and led the way through to the still room in which were two huge copper stills, shaped like giant retorts, with copper tubes coming out of them and going into large cylinders. Another man of the same age and dressed in the same way was checking gauges and peering through a porthole window in one of the stills. The nearest one was larger than the other.

'This is Jerry and he's keeping a close watch on the process right now.'

He pointed to the larger of the two stills. 'You see we distil twice, that's why there are two stills. The first is called the wash still. The washback that we talked about next door goes into this and it's heated by piped steam from a remote boiler, that goes through a pan in the bottom of the still. A still, you see, is just like a big kettle. The spout, that pipe that comes out and then angles downwards, is called the lyne arm. It then goes into the big condenser and then into the collecting receptacles. This takes about four hours and the resultant liquid is called low wine. It is about 25 per cent alcohol.'

Penny started making a diagram and jotting notes around it.

'If this was a wee home still instead of a condenser it would go into what they call a worm. The tube would be curled round and round, so that it would cool down the spirit.'

'Thank you, that's useful to know.'

'The second smaller still is called the spirit still. The low wine goes in here and is turned into whisky, with a strength of about 60 per cent. This is done slowly and carefully and takes about eight hours.'

'This is the bit I'm most interested in,' said Penny. 'My chemistry is a bit rusty, but I understand that there are different alcohols and my inspector said to ask you about something called the foreshot.'

Keith absently reached up and smoothed down his thinning hair. 'Aye, that is important. Basically, methanol evaporates at 65 degrees centigrade, so it comes off first. Ethanol, the good stuff that we want, comes off at 78 degrees. Then, when you've distilled out most of the alcohol towards the end of the run, you get the congeners and aromatics that add to the taste and give your whisky its uniqueness. The trouble is, too many of them and you'll spoil it. For this reason we have cuts where we switch from the three parts. That is the skill of the stillman, like Jerry there, knowing when to make the cuts. The foreshot is a relatively quick one, but that's got the methanol and the methyl aldehyde, the bad stuff. The middle cut we call the heart and the last cut is the feint.'

'So the foreshot is the dangerous stuff? It's full of methanol?'

'That's right, but we take measures to separate them. See the pipes going from the condenser into those closed tanks? The foreshot is collected in the spirit safe. See those windows with hydrometers inside the chambers? They measure the density of the liquid and we can compare colour charts and work out the constituents. By law it has to be locked so that no one can taste the methanol. Then the flow is altered and the heart, the good stuff, collects in the spirit receivers and then the last part, the feint, collects in the spirit safe.'

'What about someone with a makeshift still, how would they go about making the cuts?'

Keith laughed. 'By luck. Some believe that you can use the spoon test. To do that you would pour some into a spoon and set it on fire. The theory was that a safe spirit burns with a blue flame, but a tainted one with methanol would burn with a yellow flame. I've also heard that if folk use an old car radiator as a condenser then the lead in the spirit would burn with a red flame. Apparently they used to say red makes you dead.'

Penny grimaced. 'That doesn't bear thinking about. Sort of like Russian roulette.'

Keith nodded. 'That's what we think, that those poor kids had badly stilled peatreek. Is that the case?'

Penny chewed the end of her pen and shrugged. 'I'm afraid that I can't answer that. It is under investigation.'

'We're all devastated, you know. Brock Spiers is a friend of mine. He worked at Glen Corlin distillery until he had an accident. He's in a wheelchair and now Vicky is missing. It isn't fair.'

'No, it isn't. But we're doing what we can.'

'Aye, two of our lads are helping on the search, as is Hamish.'

Penny tapped her notebook. 'Then what do you do with the foreshot? Do you throw it away?'

Keith shook his head. 'No, we re-use it. It goes back into the low wine receiver and gets distilled again.'

Penny frowned. 'But isn't that dangerous?'

The head distiller shook his head. 'The aromatic substances and all the volatile substances go through catalysed reactions with the copper and they are made safe. They ultimately help with the taste. They help to make it unique. It's part of the magic of whisky making.'

The station had been quiet for about an hour, which had given Ewan the opportunity to catch up on his paperwork, tidy the rest room and fix the table tennis net. In essence he was finding work to do to stop himself from thinking about DC Penny Faversham.

She's a bonny lassie, right enough, but why would she look at you, you silly fool, he chided himself. *Just be polite, think before you speak and don't say anything stupid.*

But it wasn't easy. Although he'd only known her a couple of days, difficult days with all that was happening, he looked forward to the odd moments when he could sit and drink tea with her or explain the systems in the station or the way things were organised in Scotland.

He was daydreaming again when the bell in the outside office rang and he heard the door open and close. He went through, a pencil in his mouth and a ream of paper for the printers in his hand.

'Ah, Ewan, I was hoping to see Sergeant Driscoll,' said Stan Wilkinson, with a nervous smile on his lips. He was wearing a waterproof poncho that dripped water onto the floor.

'Still in your shorts, I see, Stan. I'm afraid she's not in. She's still managing the search.'

The postman's face registered disappointment. 'Are you on your own then?'

'Aye, manning the fort as usual. I'm getting a bit stir crazy if the truth be told. All the others are out on cases.'

'Cases? Is there a lot going on? Apart from the search, I mean.'

'Police matters, Stan. I can't say more than that.'

'Oh, of course. Stupid of me. I was just hoping that the sergeant had finished with my phone.'

Ewan picked up the phone. 'I'll give her a bell and ask her now.'

Stan turned and read the notices on the pinboard while Ewan talked to Morag. He turned when he heard the constable put the phone back on the receiver.

'Sorry, Stan. She says that while we are still investigating we need to keep it. But as soon as we can we'll release it.'

Stan scratched his beard and nodded understandingly. 'No problem. Let's just hope the girl turns up soon.'

Charlie McDonald had been receiving reports about Catriona's progress twice a day from his ex-wife Bridget. On each telephone conversation she castigated him for not being there, for never having been there for her.

He took her latest call.

'I've always been a good dad to Catriona,' he said. 'That's why I work so hard, to give her the life she deserves.'

'Whatever, Charlie! At least she's off that machine now and her vision seems to be slowly improving. She can't make out features, but she can see outlines now.'

'I'm going to find out where she got that gut-rot whisky,' he said angrily. 'And when I do —'

'There you go again! The big man and the things you're going to do.'

'Bridget, listen —'

'No, I'm tired of listening to your pompous threats. I'll call tomorrow.'

'Bridget!'

His mobile went dead as she rang off, leaving him staring at the small blank screen.

'Well, at least Catriona is getting better,' Helen whispered behind him as she ran her hands over his bare chest and brushed the back of his neck with her lips. 'Now where were we?'

Charlie laughed as he turned and leaned over her to kiss her. 'We're in your Land Rover Discovery, our love wagon as you like to think of it, when we were just rudely disturbed by my shrew of an ex-wife.'

'We'd better be quick then, we both have things to do,' she said as she circled his neck with her arms. 'And we still have to decide what we're going to do about our dirty little secret.'

The killer had been rattled when news of the girl's trainer came out. A second bloody mistake that had escaped attention, which could prove extremely costly. If only there wasn't so much to do, so many things to attend to.

Bloody Calum Steele and his rag. And that bitch that had given him all these ideas about social media and the whole bloody digital world.

He could be stopped, though. Him, his pathetic newspaper and his girlfriend.

No, wait. Perhaps it would be too soon, but if he crossed the line again and caused further inconvenience, then it would have to be bye-bye time. For him and his woman.

And that in itself would necessitate another killing.

The thought was cheering. Slightly intoxicating, if the truth be told.

But first, the girl. Another mistake would be fatal. The plods might just happen on a link and they had to be put off. The weather had been fortuitous in that it had concealed things so far, but winds would come, to clear the mist and fog. Everything needed to be done before that.

No, best to carry on with the plan. It's my move this time. And it will have to be a good one. It's obvious what needs to be done now.

CHAPTER TWELVE

The mist was still thick as Torquil rode out to the Glen Corlin Distillery on the Bullet via the Strathshiffin Road layby, where the Kyleshiffin mobile library van was parked. He could barely see any of the search party as visibility was poor, but Morag told him that she was getting reports from each group by phone every half hour.

'I'm really worried, boss. I'm losing searchers hand over fist as they all have work to do and everyone is getting tired. I've been keeping Lumsden informed, of course, but he's threatening to come over and take charge personally. He says I'm making a pig's ear of this and that it's all your fault.'

Torquil rolled his eyes. 'You're not making a mess of it at all, Morag. The weather is against us. I guess he's saying you've had a poor example over the years with me.'

'That's about it, boss.'

'Well, you'd better not call me if he does come over. I can't say it would be a joy to see the old fool.'

Morag made no comment. 'Anyway, how are the Spiers taking it? Was it definitely Vicky's trainer?'

Torquil shook his head. 'Not well, as you'd imagine. And it is her trainer, right enough.' He told her the details of his meeting with the couple.

'I wish we could find her,' said Morag. 'I'm so worried that we're just going to find a body. I hate to think of her dying of methanol poisoning somewhere out here, all alone.'

'We must keep on, Morag. She has to be somewhere, alive or dead.'

Morag heaved a sigh. 'Is there any more headway with the peatreek?'

'Wallace phoned me a wee while back. They have tracked down the local stills and confiscated whisky. Naturally enough, we've got several worried men although none of them admits to having supplied Robbie. So the supplier may still be out there. Penny is over at Hamish McNab's Abhainn Dhonn distillery and I'm on my way to Glen Corlin. We need to make sure that none of their foreshots could have found their way into these two bottles of peatreek. I'd better be on the way. Lots to do and time is marching on.'

The twin pagodas of the Glen Corlin distillery protruded eerily above the thick blanket of ground mist that shrouded the buildings as Torquil rode down the long drive on the Bullet, the headlight cutting a swathe through the mist.

The Glen Corlin pagodas were distinctive landmarks on West Uist. Each of them originally housed a Chinese-style Doig ventilator, but when the distillery stopped malting its own barley they became redundant and were kept for their aesthetic appeal and because they were symbolic of traditional whisky distilling. A picture of them adorned every bottle of Glen Corlin single malt whisky that left the distillery.

George Corlin-MacLeod welcomed Torquil into the luxury kitchen of the mansion.

'It's really my wife that deals with the distillery processes,' he explained as he poured coffee for them both. 'She doesn't exactly do any of the distilling, of course, but her family have been in the business for generations and she knows exactly how each whisky is produced. Me, I'm just the marketing man.' He smiled. 'And as your uncle may have told you, I'm also a golfer.'

Torquil nodded non-committedly as he accepted his coffee and sat down at the island in the centre of the kitchen.

'Is Esther around then?'

George shrugged as he stirred his coffee. 'We don't really keep tabs on each other, Inspector.' He gave a thin, unconvincing laugh. 'She has her distillery team well trained and the place works like clockwork.'

Torquil looked through the large window. 'The car park is pretty quiet today.'

'The weather isn't great and the whisky tours from the islands tend to be Thursday through to Sunday. This is the quiet part of the week.'

A large Land Rover Defender pulled into the private drive and Esther Corlin-MacLeod jumped out and walked briskly towards the house.

'Ah, it looks as if I'll be able to ask her soon,' Torquil said.

The sound of a door opening and closing was followed by leather boots walking across a parquet floor.

'Esther, I have Inspector McKinnon in the kitchen,' George called out.

There was a pause and then the footsteps sounded again and Esther Corlin-MacLeod walked into the room. She kissed her husband lightly on the cheek and then beamed at Torquil as if he was a long lost friend.

'This is an unexpected pleasure, Inspector McKinnon. What brings you to our humble abode? Is George looking after you?'

She looks flushed, Torquil thought. As if she has something to hide. And there is definite strain of some sort between them.

He smiled. 'Some technical information actually. You know about the three teenagers?'

Esther looked suddenly pained. 'Oh, I'm heartbroken about it. They'd been drinking, hadn't they?'

'Yes, peatreek, we think. Either that or whisky tainted with methanol. So, I just need to make sure that methanol from foreshots, either from your distillery or from Hamish McNab's, couldn't have found its way into the bottle they were drinking from.'

Both Esther and George looked surprised.

'Utterly impossible,' replied Esther. 'At least, impossible to have come from here. Who can say about McNab's tinpot outfit.'

'Why is it impossible?'

'Because we recycle it entirely. I can show you if you want to follow me over to the distillery.'

'That would be very helpful,' Torquil replied, standing and finishing his coffee. He decided he would explore why she referred to Abhainn Dhonn as McNab's tinpot outfit. Clearly there was ill feeling between them.

Penny was first to arrive back at the station and was greeted by the aroma of cooking wafting through from the kitchen.

'Hello, Ewan, something smells good,' she called as she lifted the counter flap. 'I'm starving. I'd better go and buy a sandwich from the baker.'

Ewan came out of the little kitchen with a wooden spoon in his hand. 'You're welcome to share some soup and oatcakes with me, Penny.' Then eyeing her with concern, he said, 'That is, if you're not a vegetarian. It's oxtail soup you see, but if you are vegetarian I could do you beans on toast.'

Penny laughed. 'I should be vegetarian if I'm honest, especially as I'm a nature lover. I have a struggle with the moral issue about killing animals, but I do like meat. It's not much of a compromise, but I avoid eating meat two days every week.'

'Is today a meat day then?' Ewan asked, hopefully.

'It is.'

'Good, I'll have the oxtail whipped up in a jiffy.'

'Add one slice of toast and some beans as well and I'm all yours.'

Ewan's smile froze and colour rose in his cheeks. He shuffled from one foot to the other. 'Aye, well, no bother — Penny.'

As he backed into the kitchen she screwed her eyes and punched the side of her head.

Shit! Me and my mouth. Do I tell him I didn't mean anything or — do I just leave it at that?

She was about to follow him to explain when the bell went and the door opened. She went back through to the counter as Wallace and Douglas came in, dressed in their fisherman's waterproofs. Each was carrying a large fishing crate full of assorted bottles.

'We've got a different catch today, Penny,' Wallace said. 'And we've another two in the van.'

'Are these from the stills?' Penny asked, lifting the flap for them to come through.

They put them through into the rest room and slid them under the table tennis table. 'Aye, we confiscated bottles from four stills. We've got them all listed and labelled and the names of the distillers. You can have a look while we go and bring in the others.'

'You haven't tasted any of them, have you?' Penny asked.

'We're not daft, Penny,' Wallace replied.

'Although Eggy MacOnachie might say differently,' added his brother. 'I have to confess though, we had a sniff. They all have a very different nose.'

'A nose?'

'Aye,' said Douglas. 'It's fragrance or bouquet. These all vary as you'd expect, what with them being unregulated stills. That's peatreek for you. Some are very peated, others quite seaweedy.'

Wallace raised his voice. 'Is that you cooking, Ewan McPhee? You've got two starving men here, any chance of putting on more of whatever it is you're cooking there?'

Ewan put his head round the door. He was still flushed. 'I'll open another tin of soup and another tin of beans. Penny and me were just about to —'

'Oh, don't let me and my ugly brother be gooseberries then,' said Wallace with a grin. 'We can go to the chip shop.'

'We'll just get the other crates and go,' added Douglas, beaming suggestively at Penny.

'Och, you scunner, don't be silly. We were just having a bit of food together, as colleagues.'

'That's right,' agreed Penny. 'Just as colleagues, so please join us.'

As the twins went out for the crates Ewan smiled bashfully. 'You'll get used to that pair. They like a joke, you see.'

Penny nodded. 'It happens in stations all over, Ewan. Women officers are used to it.'

'Well, you won't catch me making jokes like that,' he said, returning to the kitchen.

Damn. That's what I assumed, Penny thought, wistfully.

Torquil returned to the station to find Ewan, Penny and the Drummond twins eating and chatting in the rest room.

'Would you like some food, boss?' Ewan asked, rising from his chair.

'I could pop out and get you a sandwich if you'd prefer,' suggested Wallace.

'Or I could go to the chippie,' said Douglas. 'It would be no bother, Piper.'

Torquil shook his head. 'That's kind of you all, but I need to get my reports down on paper before I forget something. I need to think.'

Wallace and Douglas told him about their confiscation of the peatreek supplies from the four illicit stills, along with their locations and the background on the owners.

'We'll need samples getting over to the forensic lab as soon as possible.'

'Penny already asked us to get onto it, Piper,' said Wallace. 'We're going to get them sorted and off on the next ferry.'

'And I'll liaise with Ian Gillesbie and tell him they are on their way, boss,' added Penny.

'Good work, folks,' Torquil said as he retired to his office. He had just sat down when his mobile went off. It was Lorna calling from the Stornoway office.

'Hi darling,' she said. 'I'll have to be quick because Superintendent Lumsden is on the war path and he's in a rush to catch the ferry over to West Uist. You need to know that he's given an interview to Scottish TV and BBC Alba about him personally going to West Uist to take over the search for Vicky Spiers.'

'That was predictable,' Torquil replied.

'Anyway, he's given me a stack of things to do before he leaves and I'm going to be roped up for a while. He's given me a bit of a roasting for spending so much time on your case rather than on what he calls "proper policing". But this is important and I thought the sooner you know about it the better.'

Torquil pulled a writing pad closer to him. 'Shoot, Lorna. I'll make notes.'

'I talked with Dr Lamont. He's done the post-mortem on Robbie Ochterlonie. He would have talked to you, but since he already had my number and I attended the Jamie Mackintosh post-mortem, he contacted me.'

'Sounds perfectly reasonable.'

'He said that Mr Ochterlonie had died from a head injury. There were two components to it apparently. One was a blunt facial injury, which fractured his nose and produced what he called a Le Fort type 2 fracture. He explained that it's a severe facial fracture. The nasal bones splintered and the three facial bones on each side, the maxilla, the zygoma and the orbital rim were all fractured. Dr Lamont says that a fall from standing will tend to produce a type 1 Le Fort fracture, which they call a floating palate. It is a low velocity impact injury. It is not too severe, but a type 2 is called a floating maxilla. The whole of the middle of the face gets detached and pushed inwards. Effectively, the face is smashed in. It is usually associated with a high velocity impact, falling from a height or impact at speed. He reckons it was because Robbie Ochterlonie was a big man.'

'OK, I've got that down.'

'He also had a contrecoup injury to the brain. That means the back of the brain was all bruised.'

'Does that mean he was hit on the back of the head?' Torquil asked quickly.

'No, it's French, as in *contre coup*, meaning the other side. The brain effectively bounced from the trauma and hit the back of the cranium. It is consistent with a Le Fort fracture type 2.'

'What caused the fall though? Was there any evidence of a heart attack, or a stroke?'

'He thinks he had a fit. There were petechial haemorrhages inside his brain and on the surface of it. They are tiny bleeds, but all over the place. He can't say whether the fit occurred causing him to fall, or if it happened at impact as he fell. He wants to gather all the biochemical findings and the toxicology before he can say conclusively, but he wanted us to know the position now. He's made a note for Ian Gillesbie the Senior Scene Examiner to liaise with us.'

'Any idea how long that's going to be, Lorna?'

Lorna laughed. 'How long is a piece of string? Sorry, but I'd better go. Superintendent Lumsden is here. I thought I'd brief you now in case I don't get time. I thought maybe you could get Penny to catch Ian Gillesbie, since she worked with him at the scenes.'

'Aye, you're probably right, especially if Lumsden is coming over to take charge of the search.'

Hamish McNab was always careful to cover his tracks. He had done so all his life even though he liked to play with fire, but being careful had thus far prevented him from actually getting burned. He considered himself a past master in the art of using people to his advantage and prided himself on finding soft spots to exploit.

He liked the mist and fog, those wonderful meteorological conditions that gave one blanket cover to come and go. It was especially to his liking when he had things to do, to take care of. Like arranging one of his clandestine meetings. This one had been arranged quickly in response to her text.

After parking his SUV in the boathouse where her old Fiat was already parked out of possible sight, he walked round and let himself into the old fisherman's cottage by the sea. It was one of the discreet properties around the island that he had acquired over the years.

She was waiting for him, drinking a bottle of lager. She had removed her work clothes and was sitting on the settee dressed in her undies. The full works, suspender belt, fishnet stockings, all the frilly stuff that turned him on. He knew that her soft spot was to act out her fantasies. Respectable care assistant and churchy-churchy lady to everyone she knew, but internally a wanton tigress. He was pleased with the way he had groomed her so that she would spy for him.

'You took your time,' she said, dangling her shoe by the toes of her crossed leg. 'Like I told you in my text, Inspector McKinnon was around at the Hydro asking questions.'

'Asking about what, Doreen?' he asked, slumping down beside her and reaching out to stroke her fishnet covered knee. 'About me?'

'No, he never even mentioned you. He wanted to know if Robbie Ochterlonie had a secret still. And he wanted to know if he could have had a secret relationship with anyone.'

'What did you say?'

'I said I didn't know about a still.'

'And a relationship?'

'I said I thought it was likely.'

Hamish nodded as he continued to stroke her knee. 'Good girl. Did he ask anything about Catriona McDonald?'

She lay the bottle on the side table and guided his hand higher up her thigh. 'Nothing at all.'

'Good, you're a great little spy, so you are,' he returned with a chuckle before kissing her bare shoulder and letting his hand be led by hers. 'How are we for time?'

'I have until five o'clock. I took care of arrangements.'

'No rush then,' he said, running a hand up her back to unclip her bra. Soon he would take her to bed. He liked to pay his debts off straight away, especially when the paying was such pleasure.

CHAPTER THIRTEEN

Ewan arrived at the station at a little before half past seven the next morning. He was surprised by the silence when he unlocked the front door.

'*Creideamh!* Did I forget to switch on the alarm last night?' he muttered to himself. 'That's careless, Ewan. You've too much on your mind.'

He grinned to himself as he thought of DC Penny Faversham. He was determined to ask her to go for a drink with him soon. But as he opened the cupboard containing the alarm control box he found that it was flashing. Puzzled, he looked up at the siren and saw that the wires leading to it had been cut.

'Stop! Police!' he called out as he flicked up the counter flap and went quickly through to the corridor and then noisily checked each room, ever ready as he did so in case the intruder was still on the premises.

The back door was closed, but the lock was damaged. Before he did anything else he pulled out his mobile phone and called Morag. She answered almost immediately.

'Sergeant Driscoll, it's me, Ewan.'

'It must be more bad news if you are using my rank. What's wrong, Ewan?'

'The station has been burgled.'

'Are you on your own? Are you safe?'

Despite himself, Ewan smiled. It was typical of Morag that her foremost concern was for him rather than the building. 'I'm fine, Morag. Whoever did it knew what they were doing. They forced the back door and then went straight for the alarm and cut the wires to the sirens. The alarm must have gone off for just a few seconds.'

'I'm on my way, Ewan. Have a look round, but don't touch anything. I'll need to dust for fingerprints. Meanwhile, call Torquil.'

It was just a matter of minutes before Morag arrived.

'Piper is on his way, too,' Ewan told her. 'And DC Faversham. I thought I should get her in to check her office.'

Morag nodded as she looked around. 'Has anything been taken that you could see?'

'A few things, but I haven't opened any cupboards or drawers in case I smudge any prints.'

'There should just be ours then. I have all of ours in my files, so I'll just need to get Penny's when she comes in. I'll get on with dusting for prints.'

She went through to the rest room and opened the cupboard where she kept the forensics kit that she used in the days before all forensics were farmed out to the Scene Examiners. Pulling on latex gloves and taking out her equipment, she asked over her shoulder, 'So what things have been taken?'

'The petty cash tin has gone and as far as I can see also the stuff relating to the teenagers. All the things that had been found on the search including the bag with the trainer that was found. And my new murder shoes, as well.'

Morag stood up and eyed him quizzically. 'Your what?'

'You know, my hammer boots. My murder shoes. And I've not even worn them yet.'

The station phone rang and Ewan went to answer it while Morag began her investigations. He was still speaking when Torquil arrived.

'I see, thank you Mr Corlin-MacLeod. We'll get someone out to you straight away. If you could just stay exactly where you are and don't disturb the ground near it that would be very helpful.'

'Is Morag in?' Torquil asked, lifting the counter flap.

'Yes, boss. She's started dusting for fingerprints, I think. But I think you need to hear this first. That was Mr Corlin-MacLeod. He was heading into Kyleshiffin to catch the early ferry when he saw something beside the road. It's an Adidas trainer.'

'So is he on the Strathshiffin Road?'

'No, he's on the west coast road.'

Torquil raised his eyebrows. 'A curious way to go, unless he wanted to go by McNab's Abhainn Dhonn distillery.'

'Do you want me to go out there?'

'No, leave this to me. You help Morag.'

Torquil rode over to the west, going past the Abhainn Dhonn Distillery and then along the West Coast Road as it chicaned before hitting a long straight section that cut through crags and gullies towards the south of the island. Up ahead, he saw the red Lamborghini Aventador Roadster SV with the personalised number plate GCM 1 parked by the side of the road with its hazard lights flashing. As he rode alongside it the doors slid open, lifting upwards like dragon wings.

Pure ostentation and totally impractical for the roads of the Western Isles, thought Torquil.

George Corlin-MacLeod got out of the supercar and waved. 'I hope this isn't a fool's errand I've brought you out on, Inspector McKinnon. I saw this and thought it looked like the trainer I saw on the *West Uist Chronicle* blog.' He led the way back down the road as Torquil pulled the Bullet onto its stand. 'There it is on the other side of the ditch.'

155

Torquil took off his helmet and goggles and followed. He jumped over the ditch to look at the shoe.

'It's covered in mud and seems to be soaked through. It's probably been there quite a while. I'm pretty certain that's the other one, Mr Corlin-MacLeod. And it looks like there is scuffing on the wall of the ditch.'

'As if she stumbled into it and it came off when she climbed out?' the distillery owner suggested.

'Possibly,' Torquil replied, pulling out his phone and taking photographs of the trainer, the disturbed mud in the ditch and the ditch itself. When he finished, he stood up, and said, 'This could be a big help. Thank you for calling it in.'

'I couldn't do anything else. Poor kid. The whole island is praying that she's all right.'

Torquil nodded and took a polythene bag out of a pocket of his leather jacket. 'I'll need to get it back to compare with the one we have at the station.'

Once he had bagged the trainer he went back to the Bullet and deposited it in a pannier, then took out a roll of police tape.

'I'm just going to mark this area as a scene, if we need to get further tests done. No need for you to stay any longer. I understand you've got the ferry to catch.'

'Aye, I have some business on Lewis.'

'You've taken the long way to Kyleshiffin though.'

George Corlin-MacLeod nodded. 'I've got a lot on my mind, Inspector. I thought a longer drive might clear my head. I've been doing that a lot lately. Escaping, you might call it. Like playing golf with your uncle.' He pursed his lips and nodded as he got back into his car. 'Well, I suppose I'd better go and catch that ferry.'

With a press of his key fob the supercar's wing doors closed, the engine fired and the distillery owner accelerated away, leaving Torquil with the distinct impression that he wanted him to know that he'd been playing golf with the Padre.

The station was full of uniformed officers when Torquil arrived back. They had been staying at the Commercial Hotel in between the daytime searches. All of them knew Torquil and they exchanged greetings with him as he let himself through the counter-flap.

Suddenly a familiar voice began shouting from the rest room.

'Superintendent Lumsden is not in a good mood, Piper,' said one of the officers, a fellow piper who played with the Lewis Pipe Band. 'He's dressing down Morag and Ewan.'

'Aye, he gave us much the same last night when he arrived at the hotel and found us having a pint in the bar,' added another, a burly officer who usually came second to Ewan in the hammer throwing events in the games circuit.

'Thanks, lads,' Torquil said, going through to find Superintendent Kenneth Lumsden addressing Morag and Ewan, who were both standing to attention. Penny Faversham was standing apart, clearly feeling very awkward.

'Never in all my years have I come across such a shambles. Your station has been burgled?'

'Good morning, Superintendent Lumsden,' Torquil said calmly.

The uniformed officer spun round, his eyes flashing at sight of Torquil. 'Ah, Detective Inspector McKinnon, you do know that you've been burgled?'

'I do, although I had to go out urgently. We've found another trainer.'

Superintendent Lumsden looked down at the bag containing the trainer. 'You're sure it is a match?'

'That's what I'm about to find out,' Torquil replied. 'I'm going to compare it —'

'Good luck with that, then. Were you listening when I said your station was burgled?'

Torquil ignored the heavy sarcasm he was used to from all his past encounters with his former superior officer. Since he was moved over to join the Criminal Investigation Department after the changes of 2013 it had been a relief to no longer be under his command.

'The trainer was among things stolen, sir,' said Morag in her best diplomatic tone. 'Along with the petty cash tin, a mobile phone, a couple of old tennis balls and various debris produced by the search. Then some torches, a couple of tins of baked beans from the kitchen, a loaf of bread and a bottle of lemonade.'

'And my murder shoes, I mean, my hammer boots,' added Ewan.

Torquil held up the bagged trainer. 'But we have photographs so we can still check it.'

He told them all where it had been found by George Corlin-MacLeod.

'Well, I've made a decision,' went on Superintendent Lumsden. 'I'm personally taking over the search. Where is this library van you say you've been using as an operational base?'

'It's parked behind the station, sir,' replied Morag.

'Right, give me a map and the exact location of the second trainer. I'm going to use that point as the new base and we'll spread out from there.'

'I've put a police tape around the area in the ditch where the trainer was found on the West Coast Road,' Torquil informed him. 'You cannot miss it.'

Lumsden snorted derisively.

'The map is in the library van, sir,' said Morag. 'I'll show you on the way.'

'You're not coming, Sergeant. You can stay here and supervise this station. Sort out this burglary and find the nutter who robbed you of your petty cash tin and the constable's hammer boots or whatever.' He looked at Ewan and shook his head. 'Constable McPhee, you'll stay, too. You can look after lost kittens and things within your capability.''

'Sergeant Driscoll has done a good job and Constable McPhee is highly capable,' Torquil said quickly. 'Don't you think you should have people who know the island?'

'The girl is still lost, isn't she?' he returned bullishly. 'It looks like she hasn't been found because you've been looking in the wrong place. I just hope it isn't a corpse that we find. You've already lost one teenager.' He turned to Morag, whose eyes were moist from holding back tears. 'Come on, Sergeant, show me that map and give me the keys of this vehicle. My officers will follow. Lastly, how have the civilians been notified?'

'We've been helped by the *West Uist Chronicle*, sir. They have been sending out emails and blogs.'

'The local rag and social media! That's how you run this place, is it? Well, if that's the best there is get onto the editor and tell him to get a message out about the new location. I'll be directing the search from there. Have we got dogs?'

'We will have, but they are civilian animals,' replied Morag. 'It was one of our islanders' dog that found the first trainer.'

'Well, I'll need the second trainer to see if they can pick up a scent,' returned the superintendent.

'I need to check it first, Superintendent,' said Torquil, holding the bag firmly by his side. 'Once I'm sure it's a match I'll get it out to you.'

Lumsden's jaw muscles twitched and he seemed on the verge of erupting, but instead he snapped, 'Do that.' He gave a bullish call to the constables waiting in the front office and then nodded at Morag to lead him out to the library van. The uniformed officers marched through quickly to follow them, grimacing sympathetically at their West Uist colleagues.

'Bloody fool!' Torquil exclaimed, after they had gone.

'I'd heard all about him from Detective Superintendent Ross,' said Penny. 'He's a typical bully boy.'

'I'm afraid he's transferred his antipathy towards me onto Morag,' said Torquil. 'But let's have a look at the photographs of the other trainer. Let's make sure it is Vicky's. If it is it gives some hope that she may still be wandering around out there.'

When Morag came back some minutes later Torquil put his arm around her shoulders. 'Don't let him get to you, Morag. You've done all that you can and we all support you.'

'I've not found her, Torquil. If she's lying dead in a ditch I'll never forgive myself.'

'Hush now, the best thing to do is to get down to the work. So let's have all we know about this break-in.'

'I've dusted and there are our prints all over, but nothing new. I don't think Penny can have been near the things that were stolen.'

'So whoever did it wore gloves and they knew what they were doing,' said Torquil. 'Quick entry then straight to the alarm and cut the wires to the sirens. The things that were stolen, do they make any sense?' He looked at the list of things that Morag and Ewan had compiled before Superintendent Lumsden descended upon them. 'It seems a pretty eclectic mix.

The worrying thing is that the stuff found on the search has been taken, especially Vicky's trainer.'

'Aye,' said Ewan. 'Is Superintendent Lumsden right? Have we some nutter on the island? I can't really think of who else would do such a thing.'

Torquil moved towards the corridor. 'I'll give Calum a ring about sending one of his emails out to tell folk that the search has been moved six miles away and ask him to tell folk where to go for the start of the new search. While I do that, Ewan please get the photographs and let's make sure about the second trainer.'

Penny knocked on Torquil's office door and came in upon his call.

At his invitation she sat down and opened her notebook. 'I've spoken to Ian Gillesbie as you told me to. He's had most of the results back and he's going to email them to me. He also said that Dr Lamont had done the histology on the tissue samples and looked over all of the results on the body fluids, so he suggested that I speak to him directly, which I did. To be honest, he was a bit curt and started off saying that he had wanted to talk to Sergeant Golspie, since he liked to have continuity.'

Torquil shrugged. 'I guess that you need to like method and order if you are going to be a good forensic pathologist.'

'Well, he said he'd give me his overall assessment, but would be writing up a detailed report for the Procurator Fiscal. Further to his post-mortem findings he said that Robbie Ochterlonie died as a result of a fall while under the influence of alcohol, both ethanol and methanol. The level of methanol in his blood was really high, probably lethal. The levels in his aqueous and vitreous humours in his eyes were also high. The stomach had probably contained a whole bottle of whisky, of high methanol content. His blood sugar was in his boots, as the result of insulin, since he was a type 1 diabetic.'

'So he'd injected himself, thinking his sugar was too high and that he could fall into a coma?'

Penny nodded. 'Possibly injecting too much and then either fallen after having a fit, or had a fit and fallen, sustaining the facial injury and the contrecoup head injury when he hit the floor.'

Torquil whistled. 'A grim way to go. So what about the peatreek samples from the stills. Did Ian Gillesbie have any information there?'

Penny turned the pages to a marker. 'Yes. None of them had anything but a negligible amount of methanol. They bore no resemblance to the liquids from the two bottles. Ian didn't think there was any chance that they came from any of those stills.'

'So it looks like the deadly still is still out there?'

Penny nodded. 'Yes, boss.'

'Ok, let me see the forensic reports when Ian Gillesbie sends them over.'

Calum and Cora wasted no time in writing another digital special, which found its way into the inboxes of people's emails all over the island.

It read:

THIRD DAY AND STILL NO VICKY
SECOND TRAINER FOUND
SEARCH MOVED

Then followed details of the trainer and its location on the West Coast Road along with the invitation to join the search under the direction of Superintendent Kenneth Lumsden.

One of the first to read the blog, the killer smiled.

Torquil refused Ewan's offer of tea.

'I think I need some air, Ewan. I'll go for a ride on the Bullet and I'll be back soon. I'm on my phone if you need me.'

It was not long after he had gone that Penny came out of her office, only to be greeted by Ewan bearing a tray with mugs of his strong, near stewed tea. She suppressed a grimace and accepted it with a smile.

'Did I hear the boss go out?' she asked.

'Aye, Penny. He's gone for some air.'

Morag came through and took a mug. 'He had that look on his face,' she volunteered. 'You'll get to recognise it, Penny. It's a pensive one, so I expect he's gone to do what he does when he has a problem.'

'What exactly is that?'

'He's gone to play his pipes,' Morag replied.

Which is exactly what Torquil had done. He had ridden the Bullet out to St Ninian's cave and crunched his way over the shingle to play in the cathedral-like cavern. He was troubled. More troubled than he had been for a long time, not just because of the pillbox tragedy, but because something was not right.

In the cave he began to play his pipes. He played a number of his favourite pieces, just as they came into his head. And as he played snatches of music, almost stream of consciousness fashion, he ran through the words of the songs in his mind.

Then he started to play Loch Lomond:

By yon bonnie banks and by yon bonnie braes

Where the sun shines bright on Loch Lomon'
Where me and my true love were ever wont tae gae
On the bonnie, bonnie banks o' Loch Lomon'

And as he played, the lyrics running through his mind, he started to get a strange prickling feeling run up and down his spine.

Oh you tak' the high road and I'll tak' the low road
An' I'll be in Scotland afore ye,
But me and my true love will never meet again
On the bonnie, bonnie banks o' Loch Lomon'

He suddenly let the blow pipe drop from his lips and he chopped the bag to silence the instrument. 'That's it. The high road and the low road. High and low!'

He left the cave, muttering his thanks to it for granting him enlightenment as he played and jogged across the shingle and seaweed to climb up onto the roadside and the layby where the Bullet was parked.

Stowing his pipes in the pannier he straddled the machine and pulled out his phone to make an urgent call to the station.

'Morag, I'm coming in shortly, but I just need to go somewhere first. Get the twins to come in, I need the old team together. Let's do what we do best.'

He hung up before she could question him further. Moments later he was opening up the throttle and accelerating along the headland road, the noise of the engine sending flocks of herring gulls seawards towards the safety of the familiar stacks and skerries.

CHAPTER FOURTEEN

'Where's Penny?' Torquil asked Morag when he returned to the station.

'She's in her office, boss. The Drummonds are on their way in. What is it? I can see you've got that look on your face.'

'I'll tell you soon, Morag. Call me when the whole team is here.'

Penny came out of her office upon hearing his voice.

'Ian Gillesbie sent through the reports, boss. I've printed them out and put them on your desk.'

'Good, that's just what I needed to hear. While I'm reading it gather all the information you have on the pillbox event and on Robbie Ochterlonie.' Turning to Morag, he said, 'When the twins arrive gather the team in the rest room. Ask Ewan to get the whiteboard ready and have different coloured marker pens and notepaper ready for everyone.'

Ten minutes later, after he had digested the reports and called Dr Ralph McLelland to ask for some medical advice, Torquil went through to the rest room where the others were waiting.

As usual, Ewan had made a big pot of tea and handed cups to everyone before they began.

Torquil took a drink of tea then went over to the whiteboard. 'Well folks, things are pretty bad as you all know, but things have just gotten a whole lot more complicated. We're going to have a brainstorming session. Penny, you take minutes and everyone else make notes as we go along.'

He tapped the whiteboard. 'Right, so we have two incidents here. The first is the pillbox where the three teenagers were drinking peatreek and having a post-exam get-together. The teenagers were Jamie Mackintosh, Vicky Spiers and Catriona McDonald.'

On the left hand side of the board at the top Torquil wrote PILLBOX and drew a square around it. Underneath he drew three circles in a row, each with an arrow pointing to the pillbox square. Inside each he wrote the name of one of the teenagers. Under Jamie Mackintosh's he put a cross and the letters RIP. Similarly, under Vicky Spiers's name he wrote 'missing,' and under Catriona McDonald's, 'hospitalised, dialysis, visual problems.'

'OK, what do we know about them?'

'They were all doing their Highers,' said Ewan.

'Jamie's dad, Angus Mackintosh is a carpenter. He was on a bender at the time,' said Wallace.

'Vicky Spiers's parents are Jeannie and Brock Spiers. Brock is disabled after an accident at the Glen Corlin Distillery seven years ago. He's wheelchair bound,' said Morag.

'Catriona McDonald's parents are divorced,' said Penny, reading from her file. 'Charlie McDonald is a local councillor and her mother Bridget has her own internet business. They share custody of her.'

Torquil added 'Student-Highers' under each teenager's circle. Then he picked up a red pen and wrote each parent's name and surrounded each with their own circle and drew arrows between them to show the relationships. He tapped Jamie's circle with the end of his pen and asked, 'OK, Jamie's post-mortem, what do we have?'

Penny summarised. 'Inhaled vomit and aspiration pneumonia. Brain and lungs showed evidence of asphyxiation. That is from little blood haemorrhages called petechiae — kidney disease called renal dysplasia. Effectively he only had one functioning kidney — high methanol level and other toxins — his blood tests showed he had metabolic acidosis.'

Below Jamie's circle Torquil added these details as a series of bullet points. 'And Catriona McDonald also had this metabolic acidosis, didn't she? Ralph McLelland treated her for it.'

He added bullet points under her circle, underscoring the methanol poisoning under both teenagers' entries.

'And she had visual problems, also undoubtedly methanol caused,' he added as he wrote. 'Ralph said it was called optic neuritis.'

Swapping marker pens again, on the top right of the board he wrote 'Lochiel's Copse' and drew a square around it. Lower down he wrote Robbie Ochterlonie's name and circled it, adding underneath the cross sign.

'What else?' he prompted.

'He was the manager of the Old Hydropathic Residential Home,' said Ewan.

'He was an ex-fisherman, like us,' said Douglas.

'And he liked his peatreek,' added Wallace.

'He was a type 1 diabetic, which means he had to take insulin,' replied Penny. 'And apparently he wanted to be a writer. He was always on his laptop, writing his novel or short stories. At least that's what they thought and what he told them he was doing.'

Torquil added bullet points with the information under his circle. Then to Penny, he said, 'First let's put down the findings at the scene, amalgamated with any tests from forensics.'

Penny turned pages in the file to the appropriate entries. 'Body discovered by Norma Ferguson on Monday morning. She had been concerned because he had not shown up for work so she went round to his cabin after breakfasts at the home had been served. Nor had either of the two teenagers, by the way. The body was lying face down in the sitting room. A whisky glass and a bottle were lying near the body and in the kitchen a couple of empty insulin bottles and a syringe were lying on the table along with his mobile phone. The bottle contained illicitly distilled whisky. It exactly matched the residue found in the bottle the teenagers had used.'

Torquil jotted more bullet points under the title 'Scene findings'. Once he had finished he asked Penny, 'What about his laptop?'

She shrugged her shoulders. 'There wasn't one in the cabin.'

Torquil raised his eyebrows momentarily, then went on. 'Yesterday, Lorna reported the main post-mortem findings to me. Dr Giles Lamont said that he sustained a blunt facial injury called a Le Fort type 2. This effectively means that the middle of his face was shoved inwards. It is usually caused by a high velocity injury, like a fall from a height rather than a fall forward onto the face. The latter apparently causes a Le Fort type 1 or floating palate injury, which is not as severe.

'The post-mortem also showed a contrecoup injury, that is injury to the back of the brain as it bounced back and struck the inside of the cranium. That too is consistent with a high velocity injury. Also, there were petechial haemorrhages over his brain, which implied he'd had a convulsion. Whether that was before he fell or after he'd struck his head is not clear. The pathologist wasn't sure.'

He jotted the information further down the board as bullet points under the title 'Post-Mortem Findings'. Then he picked up the typed out reports that Penny had given him and looked at notes he had jotted down in the margins.

'The next points come from testing of the blood samples that Ralph McLelland took and also the ones from the post-mortem. Dr Lamont also took samples of the stomach contents and body fluids, including from his eyes. First, he had high, toxic and almost certainly lethal levels of methanol in all of these. They use testing called head space gas chromatography with a flame ionisation detector and they can work out all of the toxins in his system. It was predominantly methanol in his case as death occurred soon after. The blood results also showed extremely low blood sugar.' He added the notes about these findings as another series of bullet points. 'What does that mean to you?'

Penny raised her hand and pointed to the board. 'There were two empty insulin bottles, one fast-acting insulin and the other long-acting insulin. And an empty syringe.'

'So presumably he'd recently taken a big dose of insulin?' suggested Morag.

'Aye, insulin drops the blood sugar, so it would show a low blood sugar right enough,' said Wallace.

'And a low blood sugar like that along with a skinful of peatreek, never mind whether it is methanol or good ordinary whisky would make him wobbly legged to say the least,' Douglas said, nodding his head in agreement with his brother.

Torquil circled the methanol readings in all of the tests with a green marker. Beside them he wrote in capital letters — HIGH.

'Look at that, we are all agreed, the readings were high. But look at this,' he said, exchanging marker pens and circling the blood sugar in black marker and beside it writing in capital letters — LOW. He tapped them both. 'High and Low!'

Morag stroked her chin pensively. 'I can't see what you are getting at, Piper. The pathologist and the forensics haven't flagged anything up, have they? It fits, doesn't it? He drank, felt his sugars going up so took a big dose of insulin then collapsed, maybe having had a fit.'

Torquil sucked air through his lips. 'Something didn't seem right to me, which is why I went to St Ninian's cave for a play on my pipes. I was just playing pieces at random and when I came to Loch Lomond it struck me.'

Ewan began to sing the words, 'You take the high road and I'll take the low road and I'll…'

'That's it,' Torquil interrupted. He tapped the two words High and Low again. 'High and low. High methanol and low blood sugar. I rang Ralph McLelland about it and he agreed, there is an anomaly. Alcohol *lowers* your blood sugar. I asked if it would even do that in a diabetic and he said that methanol certainly would.'

'So taking insulin would lower it still further?' Penny asked.

'It would,' agreed Torquil, 'but my point is that Robbie Ochterlonie was a diabetic and he'd recognise if he was having hypoglycaemia, or low blood sugar. Even drunk, he would know that insulin would make it worse and he would have gone for sugary drinks, chocolate, anything sweet instead. What he wouldn't have done is take insulin and certainly not as much as he apparently took.'

The news evoked surprise in everyone in the room.

'After taking so much insulin it is doubtful that he would have made it through to the sitting room and drunk more peatreek. But there is more to say. Dr Lamont took several swabs at the post-mortem. I have the results in the report Penny obtained from Ian Gillesbie. There was spermatozoa in his urethra.'

Morag frowned. 'Does that mean anything, Torquil? As I understand it ejaculation can occur at death.'

Torquil nodded. 'Aye, it can occur, I believe. But swabs were also taken and the lab found condom lubricant oils on the swabs from the shaft of the penis. It looks as if he had sex soon before death and he was wearing a condom.'

Penny urgently started flicking through the pages in her file. After a few moments, she said, 'There were no condoms either used or unused found in the cabin, boss. All the bins were gone through, of course.' She tapped her pen on her file. 'And I don't think the tests reported any evidence of body fluids from a sexual partner on him?'

'If he was wearing a condom there wouldn't necessarily be any,' Torquil pointed out.

Ewan winced. 'This is looking bleak, boss.'

'So he wasn't alone when he died?' Penny asked.

'Was this person male or female?' Douglas asked. 'Is there any way of knowing?'

Torquil shrugged. 'That I don't know. But if there was a second person, then it explains things. Like the blunt injury, this Le Fort type 2 facial fracture. It's possible that someone threw him down or ground his face into the floor. And it could explain the insulin. He may have been given the insulin after getting very drunk. I talked all this over with Ralph McLelland and he thinks this is all plausible.'

Penny stared at Torquil in horror. 'Gosh, I'm sorry, boss. I didn't have any suspicions that there was another person present.'

'Nor was there any reason to suppose so from the facts. But it begins to look like murder. Especially when two things aren't here that should be. No condoms and no laptop. Remember, he wanted to be a writer, but there is no laptop recorded here in the cabin.'

He added the words 'no condoms' and 'no laptop' under the scene findings label and drew stars beside them. He picked up his tea and took a sip. 'I'm going to have to talk with the

Procurator Fiscal about it all, which is why we need to get our ideas together first. So, with the knowledge that the two bottles contained the same composition of peatreek it is likely that they came from the same illicit source.'

With a green marker pen he wrote in capital letters the word 'WHISKY' at the top of the middle section of the board. Halfway down he wrote the word 'Peatreek', and then enclosed them both in squares. From the peatreek square he drew arrows to the pillbox and Lochiel's Copse squares and then to each of the teenagers and to Robbie Ochterlonie.

'We have two bona fide distilleries on the island; Abhainn Dhonn and Glen Corlin,' he said.

Under the label 'whisky' he put the names of the two distilleries in circles and inserted arrows from the whisky square to each distillery. Below each one he wrote the names of the owners and of the people who worked at them.

'So you'll need the names of the four illicit peatreek still owners,' said Wallace. 'Tosh MacNeill, Larry Kennedy, Norman Smith and Drew McQueen. Drew is a crofter and the others are fishermen. We confiscated their stuff. They were the only stills we could find out about.'

'We'll need their peatreek analysing as soon as possible,' Torquil replied as he added their names under the peatreek box.

'Don't forget that Catriona McDonald and Vicky Spiers worked at the Hydro,' said Morag.

Torquil nodded and made a new square for The Old Hydropathic Residential Home and under it added their names and those of Norma Ferguson, Doreen McGuire and Millie McKendrick. He added arrows from the two teenagers' circles to the Hydro box.

'It's quite a tangled web already,' Penny said.

'Aye, or a skeleton framework. Now we need to add flesh to the bones. Photographs, we want all the ones you've all taken. Print them out and stick them up here.'

'I forwarded the ones from Stan Wilkinson's phone and already printed them out, Torquil,' said Morag. 'They're in my drawer.'

'Ah yes, Stan Wilkinson,' said Torquil. 'He took Catriona to hospital and he also found and took Angus. We'll put him on the board, too.' He added the postman's name to the bottom left of the board and circled it, then added arrows to Angus Mackintosh and to Catriona McDonald. Underneath it he wrote 'Good Samaritan'.

Ewan suddenly smacked himself on the forehead. 'Boss, I just realised, the burglary! Stan Wilkinson's phone was among the things that were taken from the station. And among the other bits and pieces were things that Morag's search team had found.'

'Including Vicky's trainer,' agreed Morag.

'And my murder shoes,' Ewan added. 'They were brand new and unworn.'

Torquil made another list under the title 'Burglary' and drew an arrow between Stan Wilkinson's name and the mobile phone and between Vicky's trainer and the pillbox. He continued, 'When I interviewed the staff at the Old Hydro Millie McKendrick told me she suspected that Robbie Ochterlonie may have had a secret relationship. She also thought that Norma Ferguson had a soft spot for him. Then Doreen McGuire said she thought she might be right about that.'

He added the words 'secret lover' to the right of Robbie's circled name then underlined it twice for emphasis. Then he added a question mark and an arrow between Norma Ferguson and Robbie and a larger question mark beside the 'secret lover'.

'So, the first question is whether his secret lover is also his secret killer? The second arises if we conjecture that there is more than coincidence about the two events being linked, because the same peatreek was consumed in both cases.'

'It all puts a different light on our search too, Torquil,' said Morag.

'Exactly,' Torquil replied with a nod of his head as under Vicky's circle he added the words 'alive or dead?' He looked round the room. 'Or, which seems increasingly likely, as we have found no sign of her apart from two trainers found six miles apart from each other, is she being held somewhere against her will?'

Torquil left the others to reflect on the board while he went through to his office to make calls. He talked the cases over with Josephine Pengelly, the Procurator Fiscal in Oban, updating her on the search for Vicky Spiers and outlining his concerns about the death of Robbie Ochterlonie. She agreed that there was urgency now in finding Vicky Spiers and also discovering the source of the illicit whisky. The pillbox inquiry was now a potential culpable homicide case, because of Jamie Mackintosh's death, but possibly also one of abduction in the case of Vicky Spiers. She also agreed that Robbie Ochterlonie's death was highly suspicious and that it should now be considered a murder investigation.

Detective Superintendent Ross listened and agreed on Torquil's conclusions and his proposed plans of action and asked to be kept briefed on all developments.

Both Josephine and DS Ross agreed that he needed to go public on the way the cases were opening up, so Torquil phoned Calum. Both he and Cora were busy writing articles for the next edition of the *Chronicle*.

'It's bad news, Piper. So you think that poor Robbie was murdered?'

'Aye, and there is a strong possibility that whoever murdered him is also responsible for poisoning the youngsters at the pillbox. That may mean that they may also have abducted Vicky and be holding her against her will.'

'Have I your blessing to write it all up, using these terms? As you know, I am not one given to scare-mongering, but this is huge.'

'You have carte-blanche, Calum.'

'Then the *West Uist Chronicle* is at your service. We'll not let you down, Piper. Oh, and by the way, pass on our best wishes to your fiancé.'

As Torquil put the phone down he realised that Calum had just put in his best man bid. It had inevitably gone out of his mind the last few days and he felt guilty about even thinking of anything else other than the cases in hand, both of which had taken momentous leaps in importance.

His next phone call was to Kirsty Macroon at the Scottish TV newsdesk. As before, they recorded the interview on Torquil's iPhone, which he then emailed to her.

Following that, he talked with Fearghas Mac an Fhilidh at BBC Alba, the Gaelic language television channel based in Stornoway and after that, with Donald McGregor at the BBC Scotland newsdesk in Glasgow.

Finally, he went back through to the rest room, to find the others clustered around the table tennis table looking at batches of freshly printed photographs of the pillbox, Jamie Mackintosh's body, Robbie Ochterlonie's cabin and his body, and all the other photographs appertaining to each case.

'We were just seeing what we have before we stick them up, Torquil,' said Morag.

He nodded. 'Good, we want everything up here. I've talked to Superintendent Ross and with Josephine Pengelly and they both agree and know that I'm starting a murder enquiry to run alongside the search for Vicky Spiers. I'm calling this an abduction case. Do you want to tell Lumsden or shall I?'

A half smile crossed Morag's lips, followed by an emphatic shake of the head. 'Much as I'd like to, I think I'm in enough trouble with him as it is. Do you mind, Torquil?'

'No problem. It doesn't need to be a long call as I've too much to do now. I'll tell him he needs to start knocking on doors.'

Calum and Cora had wasted no time at all.

'Short, pithy and prompt, that's what we have to be with these bulletins, Cora. We have to keep ahead of the big TV stations, but remember that we are the main information stream for the island. These little pieces will have everyone eager for the actual paper copy tomorrow. Are you ready?'

'It's all loaded up, master.'

'Then press the button, lassie.'

Moments later, across West Uist the messages, texts and emails beeped, buzzed and rang out, with the three line message in capital letters:

**PIPER MCKINNON SAYS ROBBIE OCHTERLONIE
WAS MURDERED
HAS VICKY BEEN ABDUCTED?
SEARCH FOR THE DEADLY STILL**

As before, readers were given the link to the *West Uist Chronicle* blog and the details of the cases.

The killer read the *West Uist* piece with mounting anger. So the plods had stumbled onto something. Planting the second trainer far from the first seemed to have worked. A Super Plod had come over to the island to take over the search, but what could he possibly have found to make the quantum leap about Ochterlonie?

Bugger! Bugger! Bugger!

There was only one thing for it now.

The kid had to be terminated, like the other one.

CHAPTER FIFTEEN

'We need the census records, Penny,' said Torquil. 'We need to know who owns or rents every house, barn, shed and chicken shack on the island. Morag, you'll need to hold Lumsden's hand on this, so I'll leave you to liaise with him once we have a listing of all habitations in the area of the first search.'

'Onto it, boss,' said Penny, making for her office.

He snapped his fingers. 'Ah yes, also do some research about methanol. Ralph McLelland said that a lethal dose would be something like 30 mls. And that 10 mls would be enough to affect vision. But normal alcohol counters it, so it would have to be a whole lot more in a bottle to produce that effect. It's making me doubt that these peatreek bottles just happened to contain an unfortunately large amount of foreshot. I'm thinking they were deliberately loaded with methanol. Find out where it can be obtained. Maybe look at where fatalities have occurred.'

Penny stared wide-eyed for a moment then nodded and turned on her heel to her office.

'Wallace and Douglas,' Torquil said, 'I want you to check out Robbie's cabin. I want you to look for any loose floorboards, hidden panels, anywhere that he might have stored his peatreek.'

'OK, Piper. And if we find anything?' Wallace asked.

'Let me know straight away. I'm going to the Old Hydro to see if the laptop is there. I suspect it won't be, though. I think the killer or the secret lover will have taken it to destroy incriminating evidence.'

The leg was painful, but Angus was in no mood to allow it to stop him. He'd swallowed several painkillers and washed them down with a mouthful of cold tea. By choice he would have done so with whisky, but he needed to be cold sober. Apart from that, he had lost the taste for the stuff after Jamie's death.

He had wheeled out Jamie's mountain bike and rode with some difficulty, but with less pain than he would had he walked. Walking had not been an option, of course, as it was too far from his cottage. The car was also not an option, even if he had gone to collect it, because he didn't want the sound of its engine to alert the bastard that he was coming. Fortunately, the shop was at the far end of Kyleshiffin and the fog and mizzle were still limiting visibility.

As it was, he arrived at the destination and thought that it looked deserted. The shop had a closed sign on it as did the smokery next door. Nonetheless, he was determined to do what he had planned. He was wearing his work utility belt, with his chisels, screwdrivers and hammer.

He went round the back of the smokery to the sheds that adjoined it. In a matter of moments, he had opened the door and stepped inside.

So I was right! This is where you make the stuff, you evil bugger.

There was a crate of unused bottles and two crates of plain unlabelled bottles full of amber liquid.

He looked at the still and gritted his teeth. It was an old but clearly well worked apparatus, consisting of a large copper pot the size of a washing-machine raised up on a heavy trestle table. A bulbous section at the top led to the spout which fed into a coiled tube that connected with a collecting apparatus of some sort. Underneath the trestle was a large tank, which was itself connected to pipes leading into the shed from the smokery next door.

'So this is how you heated it up, from the smokery. You clever sod, running a still in Kyleshiffin itself and disguising the smell of the distilling with the smell of smoking kippers.'

He pulled out a full bottle from the topmost crate and pulled out the cork.

It smelled good in one way, yet disgusted him at the same time, almost enough to make him retch.

But then he heard footsteps outside and immediately secreted himself in the shadows behind the door. He heard a curse and the door opened.

'*Cò th'ann?* Who's there —?' the man said.

He said no more as the handle of a hammer descended on the back of his head and he tumbled to the floor, knocked senseless.

Torquil was shown into the manager's office at the Old Hydropathic Residential Home by Millie and asked to wait while she went to fetch Nora. Looking around the office that had been Robbie Ochterlonie's place of work he noted that it was perhaps not as tidy as it could be. There were three large filing cabinets, presumably containing the residents' records. An archaic looking safe stood in a corner, with the name Cartwright & Sons of West Bromwich embossed on a circular brass plate beside a large keyhole. A large pinboard was covered in resident's dietary requirements and medication lists. Beside that was a board covered in hooks with keys hanging from them. One very large antique key hung from a piece of string at the side, which Torquil had no doubt fitted the safe, clearly a relic from the days when it actually was a hydropathic hotel in the nineteenth century. However, it begged questions about the Old Hydro's approach to security. He made a mental note to tell Morag.

'Inspector McKinnon, I'm sorry, I was in the west wing. What can I do for you? Is it about the girls, or about Robbie? I saw the West Uist email and I'm shocked and heartbroken.'

'It's about Robbie, Norma. You told me he was always writing.'

'That's what he said and what he seemed to be doing. He told me he had several short stories in the pipeline and he was writing a thriller. He was always tapping away here on his laptop in odd moments.'

'What make of laptop was it, do you know?'

Norma pursed her lips. 'A Samsung, I think.'

'Did he leave it here?' Torquil asked, looking round. 'I can't see any technology other than the PC on your desk.'

'No, he always kept it with him. It's definitely not here.'

'I know it's not easy for you, but was it in his cabin when you found him?'

Norma shook her head with grimace of sadness. 'Honestly, I was too shocked to notice.'

'I understand. Did he save his work directly onto the laptop, do you remember?'

'Oh, he used memory sticks. That I definitely know.'

'Any idea where he would have kept them?'

This time she shrugged her shoulders apologetically. 'I ... I didn't know him well enough to know things like that.'

'Did anyone else here see him writing, Norma?'

'You might ask Doreen. I'll go and get her, shall I?'

'If you wouldn't mind?'

Doreen was looking pale and nervous when she came in a few minutes later. 'Norma told me to come in and see you, Inspector.'

Torquil gestured for her to sit down, which she did almost demurely. It was obvious to him that she was decidedly nervous and was avoiding eye contact more than she usually did. Her natural inquisitiveness had gone and she was not probing him for news, instead she was clearly guarded.

He leaned slightly forward and eyed her seriously. 'Doreen, I want to know about the secret lover.'

To his surprise she suddenly leaned forward and almost whispered. 'How … how did you find out? He'll be angry with me.'

Torquil raised a quizzical eyebrow. 'Who will be angry with you, Doreen?'

'Hamish McNab. Him in his position, using me to spy for him on Charlie McDonald's daughter.'

Creideamh! Torquil thought. *Now there I've uncovered a hornet's nest.* 'Hamish McNab is your secret lover and he's had you spying on Catriona?'

She looked on the verge of tears, but somehow suppressed them. 'He wanted to know anything at all about her father. Catriona liked to chat and I got quite good at probing, about his council work. I'm not sure she ever told me anything important, but Hamish liked to know. We weren't doing anything wicked. He was divorced and I — well, I've been bored.' Then she suddenly looked worried again. 'You don't need to make this public, do you? I … I'll need to talk to Hamish and to Peter, my husband. I need to prepare before it all hits the fan.'

Torquil had decided to keep up his poker face. 'I can't promise anything, Doreen. This information does not need to be made public — at least not yet. But I'm going to need you to make a statement at the station. But right now I also need to know about Robbie Ochterlonie's laptop. Did you see him writing with it?'

Doreen's eyes opened wide in surprise at the sudden change in questioning. 'Yes, lots of times. He was always on about his writing. He said he expected to become a bestselling thriller writer one day. But I think it was just fantasy.'

Torquil drummed his fingers on the desk. 'Did you see where he kept his memory sticks?'

She stared blankly at him. 'No, I'm not that great on technology. Robbie used to take the micky out of me that way. I used to just trot his own saying back to him. A word to the wise.'

Now where did I hear someone else saying that, Torquil thought. And then he remembered. 'I'd like to speak to Stuart Robertson now. Is he at the Captain's table?'

Doreen frowned. 'He's having one of his siesta days. When he has those he stays in his room and just drinks and sleeps.'

'Then show me to his room, please.'

Wallace and Douglas drove out to Lochiel's Copse and parked up beside the trailer with Robbie's boat and the pile of empty lobster pots.

'It's hard to believe that poor old Robbie was murdered in his own cabin.'

'Poor devil. It's all bizarre. Piper seems convinced he was killed by a secret lover, but I can't see that happening to someone like him.'

They ducked under the police tape and, pulling on latex gloves, entered the cabin and began a thorough search, careful to avoid the chalked outline where Robbie Ochterlonie's body had been, with the blood stains on the floor and the circled chalk marks where the glass and the whisky bottle had been found. After half an hour of thorough searching they found nothing amiss. No sign of concealed doors, cupboards or safe. No loose floorboards or hidden attic compartment.

'Nothing! No laptop. No peatreek,' said Douglas.

'So let's scout around outside.'

Back outside, they did a search of the area all round the cabin, again finding nothing. A look inside the old boat drew another blank. It was only a chance lifting of the topmost lobster pot that revealed the bottle of amber liquid inside the one behind it.

Gingerly, Wallace pulled the cork and sniffed. 'Wow! Whatever it is, it has a powerful nose.'

'Aye, but the thing is this looks like his post box, where he received his peatreek and where he kept it.'

'The question is, who was his postman?'

Stuart Robertson was in a doleful mood. He was sitting by the window of his room staring out into the fog, a mug of tea in his horny hand. Torquil could smell the fumes and had no doubt that there was more than a teaspoon of whisky in the tea.

'Stuart, why did you laugh when you told me about Robbie Ochterlonie's saying, "a word to the wise"?'

The old trawler captain stared with bleary eyes at Torquil. 'Because that's what he thought I was. One of the wise. I warned him, but he wouldn't listen.'

'Warned him about what, Stuart?'

'About lots of things. About his wheeling-dealing and his peatreek and his trysts. He thought of me as a father figure, you see.'

'Can you explain?'

Stuart took a hefty mouthful of tea and then sighed contentedly, presumably as the spirit reached his stomach. 'He liked to play with fire. He never told me exactly who with, or how, but I gather he was having a dirty affair with someone. Someone powerful, he used to suggest. Anyway, powerful enough to scare him, which is why he told me what to do if anything happened to him.'

Torquil drew up a chair close to him and leaned towards the old captain. 'He's been murdered, Stuart, you know that now.'

'Aye, I know it. I heard from Norma. And I was just debating with myself who best to talk to. If he got himself killed, why should I think that I'm safe? So I'll tell you now. He said, "Tell the police to go to Beamish Solicitors." That's exactly what he said.'

'I don't suppose he gave you anything, did he? Like a computer, or a laptop.'

Stuart's eyes seemed to clear. 'Aye, he gave me this gadget thingy for plugging into his computer. He called it his memory and said that he was trusting me, as I was his backup.'

'A memory stick, Stuart. That's what he meant. Where is it?'

The old trawler captain's eyes seemed to glaze over. 'Buggered if I can remember. I put it somewhere safe.'

Torquil silently cursed. 'That memory stick is important, Stuart. I'll need to send my Detective Constable over to search your room later. Now, you also smiled when your friend Norman said maybe you'd all find out where he got his peatreek. I think you already know who that is, don't you?'

'Ah, that is a closely guarded secret, because the distiller has kept his secret for more years than I care to think of. He supplies lots of folk here on West Uist and also all over the western Isles. In my working days I even used to help deliver them to the other isles.' He grinned. 'Now that's not going to get me in trouble, is it, Inspector McKinnon?'

'Not unless you persist in keeping it a secret.'

'Well then, like his father before him did, Archie Many Hats is the best peatreek distiller in the Western Isles.'

Douglas had taken the call from Torquil and told him about finding the bottle in the lobster pot. He reacted with surprise when Torquil then told him that Archie 'Many Hats' Reid was likely to be the secret distiller. The DI then told them to drive to his smokehouse and bring him in to the station right away, while he went to Beamish Solicitors.

The fog was still dense as the two special constables drove to the end of Harbour Street and parked outside the shop.

'Well, he's probably not in,' said Wallace. 'Looks like the shop and the smokehouse are shut up for the day. Certainly, he's not running the smokery.'

But when they went round the back they saw that the lock and bolt on one of the adjoining sheds to the smokehouse was broken and hanging down.

They both saw it and gestured at the same time to be silent. Tiptoeing to the door Wallace opened it a crack and looked inside.

'You like that, do you, you miserable sod,' said Angus Mackintosh as he poured more liquid into the mouth of Archie Reid, who was tied to the pot belly of his still, so that he was bent backwards over it. 'You killed my boy with this poison of yours.'

Wallace threw the door open and both twins entered.

'Stop right there, Angus Mackintosh!' cried Douglas in alarm. 'What are you doing, man?'

Wallace grabbed his arm and wrenched the half empty bottle from his hand.

Archie Reid gasped and laid his head backwards on the large copper spout. His cheeks puffed up and then suddenly his head shot forward and a stream of amber projectile vomit shot from his mouth, just missing the twins.

'He … he's tried to kill me,' Archie moaned.

'No more than you deserve, you bastard. You killed my boy.'

'I … I don't see —' Archie Reid said with a slurred voice as his head slumped forward onto his chest.

'*Creideamh!*' exclaimed Wallace. 'He can't see.'

Douglas was already phoning Dr McLelland.

There was no way that the girl could be allowed to live now, the killer thought. The fog was a blessing, but for how much longer. It would have to be done quickly then cleaned up and all signs of restraint removed before dumping the body.

The right footwear was important on a day like this. So important not to leave any stupid clues.

Just one more risk before leaving the bloody island for the last time. But it would be worth it so they could be properly together at last.

CHAPTER SIXTEEN

Penny had already sent an attachment about the census on an email to Torquil's phone by the time he arrived at the Beamish practice.

Only Kathleen Peterson was in the building. Torquil scrolled down the attachment on his phone as he talked to her.

'I have a list of properties around the area of Harpoon Hill and the pillbox. I hadn't realised it before, but it seems that the biggest property owners on the island are the Strathshiffin and Glen Corlin estates, Charlie McDonald, Hamish McNab and Beamish Solicitors. The list doesn't say whether the Beamish properties are occupied or not, just that they are owned by Beamish Solicitors. I need to know if there are private arrangements in place and which of the Beamish properties are occupied.'

Kathleen looked flustered. 'I'm not sure that I can divulge that information without Mr or Mrs Beamish's permission.'

Torquil did not bat an eyelid. 'I am conducting investigations into a murder and a suspected abduction. I suggest that you find this information for me now, this is urgent.'

Kathleen led the way through to her office and began working on her computer. After a few minutes she printed out a list of three properties. 'These three are unoccupied and we have no record of tenants.'

'Thank you for your cooperation. Now, where are Mr and Mrs Beamish?'

Kathleen shook her head. 'I can't tell you. Cameron Beamish is my boss and Hazie works for Helen. Hazie had to go off with a migraine after hearing the news and I have no idea

where Helen is. She had nothing in her diary. Cameron is —'
She hesitated and then shrugged her shoulders. 'I don't know
where.'

After Torquil had gone she got her mobile phone out of her
handbag and called Cameron. It went straight to answer.
Kathleen hesitated about leaving a message but decided to risk
it.

'Take care. The police have just been looking for you and
her!'

Penny had given Morag the census lists and she in turn had
sent them through to Superintendent Lumsden, who was now
ensconced in the library van overseeing the revised search. He
had given her a lambasting for working with Torquil and for
allowing him to notify the media about the change of emphasis
of the search, but after venting he had then gone into
professional mode and arranged for his officers to begin door
to doors.

Morag then took a call from Torquil, updating her on the
news about Archie Reid being the operator of another illicit
still and about Torquil's visit to the Old Hydro where he had
found out about Doreen's affair with Hamish McNab and
about the memory stick Robbie Ochterlonie had given to
Stuart Robertson. He told her to pass on the message to Penny
that he needed her to go over and help the old man find it, as
he had forgotten where he had put it. He also told her about
his visit to Beamish Solicitors where he had obtained a list of
their unoccupied properties from Kathleen Peterson in the
absence of the two partners.

After Torquil rang off Morag went through to the rest room
where Penny and Ewan were working by the whiteboard. She
told Penny about the memory stick and that he wanted her to

go over to find it in Stuart Robertson's room at the Old Hydro.

'Of course, I'll go over pronto,' Penny replied. 'But I need to add this to the board. The boss got me to do some research on methanol,' she said as she added notes to the whisky column. 'Methanol really is lethal stuff, but there would have to be an awful lot of foreshot in a bottle to make it so dangerous. The amount of foreshot produced by a small still would also be pretty small, so it would not likely be enough. That coupled with the fact that normal alcohol reduces its effect, witnessed by the fact that Dr McLelland treated Catriona McDonald's methanol overdose by giving her ethanol, suggests that those bottles must have been deliberately poisoned with pure methanol. It really isn't easy to get though.'

Morag whistled in surprise.

'There have been lots of fatal cases, but not really that many in this country, except suicides when people have taken methylated spirits. That's not what was in those bottles of peatreek. I found cases in India, Poland, Greece and Romania. Unscrupulous people added methanol to ordinary alcohol to bulk it out.'

Ewan had been looking at the whiteboard. 'Sorry to interrupt, but I keep thinking about these trainers. And my murder shoes. Do you think it could be some sort of fetishist here?'

Penny took a sudden intake of breathe. 'My God! It's been in front of my eyes all this time and I hadn't twigged it. Stan Wilkinson, he's English, isn't he?'

'Aye. He's a good fellow, always really helpful. Look, the boss called him the Good Samaritan, because he took Catriona to hospital and then Angus Mackintosh.'

Penny ran her fingers through her hair. 'He's grown a beard and he looks respectable, but I'm sure he's the same chap. I think I saw him a couple of years ago in Leeds. He was a shoplifter. He was arrested for stealing shoes. It wasn't my case, but I remember seeing the file, along with psychiatric reports. What did they say he had, some sort of thing called a paraphilia? He was a shoe fetishist!'

'*Creideamh!*' muttered Ewan. 'He seemed incredibly taken with my murder shoes. Do you think he could have been the burglar?'

'And it was his phone that was stolen with the other stuff,' said Morag. 'I sent the pictures I took at the pillbox from his phone, but maybe there were other things on the phone he didn't want anyone to see.'

'But it's been taken now,' said Penny.

'No wait!' exclaimed Ewan. 'I downloaded the whole thing to the station computer just in case.'

All three rushed through to the terminal at the front desk and watched as Ewan accessed the downloaded library. It came up as files simply numbered one to 6. Ewan opened them one by one and they showed photograph after photograph of shoes, boots, slippers of all designs imaginable. Both male and female ones. Many were just of the shoes, but others were selfies of someone wearing them, some in flesh, others with stockings, fishnets or gaudy body paints.

'I don't believe it,' gasped Ewan.

'We can't risk leaving this,' said Penny. 'Not with these cases under investigation. Do you know where he lives?'

'Aye, he rents a cottage near the Wee Kingdom,' Ewan replied.

'Then let's go,' Penny said. 'We'll go in my Mini. You direct me.'

The Wee Kingdom was a small islet of the archipelago that formed West Uist. It was a roughly star shaped peninsula facing the Atlantic on the north-west coast. With steep sea cliffs, home to thousands of fulmars and gannets, and lush well fertilised soil it was home to five self-sufficient crofts. Stan Wilkinson had been captivated by it when he first started delivering mail to the crofters and sought out the closest, affordable property that he could to it. An enquiry at Beamish Solicitors resulted in him renting an old shepherd's cottage half a mile up a twisting unmetalled road that branched off the main road before it crossed the causeway to the Wee Kingdom itself.

'Do you ever get a chance to drive without having to have the windscreen wipers on?' Penny asked as she turned off the main road at Ewan's direction.

He laughed. 'Oh, sometimes it doesn't rain for a day or two a month.' Then he winked at her. 'Only kidding, Penny. We sometimes have great weather. You've just hit a bad patch.'

She smiled back and then concentrated on driving along the pot-holed road that soon gave way to a rutted track with large muddy puddles and long tufts of grass up the middle of it, testimony to its relatively infrequent use.

'I was thinking,' Ewan said after a while. 'Maybe sometime we could, you know, maybe have a drink. If you'd like to, that is.'

Penny glanced at him and smiled as he lowered his gaze bashfully. 'I was hoping you might ask that. In fact, at lunch yesterday I was about —'

'Look! There's his van,' Ewan said suddenly as they turned a corner and saw the cottage with the Royal Mail van parked outside.

Penny parked beside the van and they got out.

'Well, at least we know he's here,' Penny said, nimbly leaping over a puddle and heading for the front door.

She knocked at the old wooden door with its equally old, flaking paint. After a few moments, when there was no reply, she tried the handle, only to find it locked.

'Maybe he's round the back,' suggested Ewan, leading the way round the cottage.

He knocked on a kitchen window as he passed and then on the door. 'Stan! It's me, Constable Ewan McPhee,' he called out. 'I'm here with DC Faversham. We need to have a word with you.'

As he tried the handle they heard a clicking noise from the other side of the house, then a creaking as a door opened. Quickly, they retraced their steps and saw Stan Wilkinson trying to walk quietly towards his van, a rucksack in one hand.

'Ah, Stan, there you are!' Ewan called.

The postman spun round and stared at them with a guilty expression on his face. 'Stay away from me. I'm going and you can't stop me.'

Penny pointed at his feet. 'What have you got on there, Mr Wilkinson?'

'My murder shoes!' Ewan exclaimed. 'So you really did burgle the station.'

Stan raised one foot six inches. 'I said stay back. These blades could be lethal and I don't want to hurt either of you.'

'Stand still!' Penny commanded. 'I know exactly who you are and I know that your name isn't Stan Wilkinson.'

'You don't know me,' he said, shaking his head vigorously and clutching the rucksack to his chest. He took a careful backward step.

'You like footwear, don't you, Mr Wilkinson?' Penny said calmly. 'I can't remember your name but it will come to me. I do remember the case file and the shoes and boots. And we've seen the photographs on your phone.'

'You can't. I've got the —'

'You've got the phone, yes, we know,' Penny replied.

'I downloaded the whole library in case Sergeant Driscoll's pictures didn't send,' Ewan said.

'So, Mr Wilkinson, I need you to come with us. I am arresting you on suspicion of burglary. You don't have to say—'

'I'm not going anywhere!' Stan cried. 'Stay back.' He raised his foot again, as if ready to kick out. Then he turned round and started to run for his van.

'Ach, do not be daft, man,' said Ewan striding quickly after him.

But before the postman had managed more than half a dozen steps the blade of a shoe dug into the ground and he tripped falling flat on his face into a deep puddle.

Ewan ran over to him. 'I'm afraid DC Faversham is right. You're under arrest.'

Morag was dealing with a holiday-maker asking for directions to the Glen Corlin Distillery when Calum and Cora came in.

'And what can I do for you both?' she asked as the tourist left.

'Give us more information, please,' replied Calum.

'We're aiming to go to press with the main paper today,' explained Cora, 'and we want to make sure we are totally up to date on developments.'

Morag quickly considered how much she could afford to tell them. The fact that they had been of so much help in mounting the search swayed her hand.

'Come through to the rest room and have a cup of tea,' she said, lifting the counter flap.

As she put on the kettle the *West Uist Chronicle* duo looked at the whiteboard.

'A real tangled skein you have there,' Calum called out over his shoulder. 'This is the sum of all your investigations, I take it.'

'It is, but you mustn't take any photographs, Calum.'

'So, do you think Robbie Ochterlonie's murder and the pillbox are all linked through the deadly still?' Calum asked. 'We're planning to run the next issue under that headline.'

Morag came through with three empty mugs, a milk jug and a biscuit barrel on a tray. 'The kettle will just take a few minutes,' she said, setting the tray down on the table tennis table. She straightened and joined them in front of the whiteboard. 'Actually, we think the peatreek bottles were adulterated with methanol.'

'Can we write this all up?' Calum asked.

'Yes, it's a murder investigation and we need any help we can get from the public.'

'That's our role, Morag. We are the conduit between the police and the public. As Torquil has said before, we are your unofficial special branch.'

Morag forced a smile, for nothing seemed humorous at this time, but she knew how susceptible to flattery of any sort Calum was. 'Aye, Calum, you two are our very special, special branch.'

'So where does this methanol come from?' Cora asked.

Morag frowned. 'DC Penny Faversham is investigating that. She's found that there were fatalities in India, Poland, Greece and Romania. She thinks —' She stopped suddenly, as if having just experienced a eureka moment. 'Actually, I need to go, folks. I know it seems a strange one, but all the others are out right now. Could I ask a big favour? Could you stay here and look after the station? Nothing will happen, just take any messages and one of us will be back soon.'

She was at the door before they could say anything.

'Help yourself to the biscuit barrel,' she called as she went along the corridor to the front office.

'Is there any sugar?' Calum called back. But all they heard was the door closing behind her.

Once inside her old VW Beetle Morag pulled out her phone to call Torquil, only to find the battery had discharged again.

'*Damnaidh!* I need to upgrade this thing,' she said, tossing it onto the passenger seat and starting up the engine.

Carrying the bottle gave a sense of power. By all accounts there was death for several people contained in it. Certainly pouring this down the kid's throat would do the job. No need to do anything different from before, just use this stuff instead of the whisky. The aim now was to terminate her rather than just subdue.

Of course, the likelihood of snuffing her out had always been on the cards, but now it had to be done. It couldn't be left any longer. It was the dumb kid's fault anyway. All of their fault.

The key made a slight rattling noise in the lock and the bottom of the door scratched on the floor as usual. He opened it and stepped inside.

Vicky had heard the noise and felt her heart pound with expectation. The cigarette lighter in her back pocket had been difficult to retrieve, but she had managed it. She had burned herself as she manipulated the lighter to burn her bonds. It had been old rope and it burned well enough for her to eventually break her hands loose. Then freeing herself had been relatively straightforward, despite the weakness and fear. It had been such a relief to unwind the duct tape that had been wound round and round her eyes and her face, leaving only room for her nose so she could breathe.

Having freed herself, she had explored the place she had been imprisoned and concluded that it had been some sort of workshop, only without any tools. She had been tied to a large heavy chair that had been bolted to the floor, which was why she had been unable to move while she was bound. Apart from that there was just an old mattress and some blankets.

But the place had only a small window high up, which was too small to escape through even if she had the strength to climb to it. And the door was securely locked and wouldn't budge.

So she had waited and waited behind the door with the only weapon she could find in her hand. A glass bottle half full of whisky.

When the man entered she moved from behind the door and swung it at his head with all the force she could muster.

It struck him on the forehead and sent him flying against the wall, stunned. He howled in pain, then cursed. She considered striking again, but the open door and the prospect of escape was too powerful. Fear drove her and she pushed past him and staggered into the fog.

She heard him roaring at her to stop, then she heard heavy footsteps running behind her.

And then ahead of her she saw a figure coming quickly towards her out of the mist, blocking her escape.

CHAPTER SEVENTEEN

Morag drove to the office of Beamish Solicitors and was told by Kathleen Peterson that Torquil had already been and gone and that he had taken the details of three properties.

'Where are Cameron and Helen?'

'Both out and neither left contacts. Shall I phone their home for you?'

Morag could see that the secretary was flustered, but she had no time to waste. She shook her head and gave her most reassuring of smiles. 'No, it will keep for another time. I'll maybe pop round tomorrow.'

She knew exactly where they lived and drove straight there, parking her car outside the high wall that surrounded their large seven bedroom home in the hamlet of Kylestradden, four miles from Kyleshiffin.

She saw Helen's BMW parked in the circular drive and made her way to the front door and pressed the bell. A few moments later, Helen answered, smiling immediately.

'Morag, what brings you here? Is the search over? Have you found poor Vicky?'

'Oh, that's a story in itself. My boss, Superintendent Lumsden, has come over from Stornoway to take over command. Could I come in?'

Helen hesitated, then stood aside. 'Of course, come through to my office. But I have to say, I am running late and can't spend much time.'

Morag followed her across the spacious hall, noting the packed suitcase by the wall.

'Are you going somewhere, Helen?' she asked.

Helen glanced at the suitcase and shook her head. 'Oh that, it's full of old clothes for the charity shop.' She gestured to an easy chair and settled herself into a plush swivel chair behind her desk. 'I just have an appointment with a client, that's all. So, what did you want to know, Morag.'

Morag smiled back. 'Your brother-in-law, you said he was a professor of chemistry in Bucharest, is that right?'

'A strange question, but yes, he is.'

'And he would have access to all sorts of chemicals, like the methanol you put into the bottles of peatreek. The one that the teenagers drank from and the other that certainly had a part to play in Robbie Ochterlonie's death.'

Helen Beamish's jaw dropped and then she gave a short laugh and sat forward, resting her hands on the desk. 'I don't believe you've just said that. It must be the strain you've been under, Morag. Your brain has blown a fuse.' She shook her head, then added, 'You do realise that I can take legal action for defamation?'

'I'm right, am I not? That you obtained methanol from Romania.'

Helen frowned. 'Where have you gotten this nonsensical idea?'

'Is it nonsensical? All those times when you kept asking me how the search was going I had thought you were genuinely concerned. What you were actually doing was making sure that we were not getting close to finding Vicky. So, tell me now, where is she?'

'You are mad, Morag. Why would I kidnap a teenage girl?'

'That's what I mean to find out and that's why I'd like you to come to the station with me right now. Inspector McKinnon will want to interview you and take a statement.'

Helen stood too, but as she did so her hand darted into a drawer and pulled out a gun. She smiled. 'How on earth you worked any of this out is irritating, but I really haven't time to waste going to the station. I'm not going to make any statement.' She nodded at the gun. 'This, by the way, is far more lethal than methanol, so just sit down and have a drink.'

Morag sat as directed, warily eyeing the gun pointed at her chest. 'I'm not thirsty.'

Helen gave a short laugh. 'Oh, I insist. You see, I have some very good alcohol that turns peatreek into a very special drink.'

With one hand she opened the drawer further and took out an unlabelled bottle of clear liquid. She pulled out the cork and set the bottle down. She poured some into a tumbler and pushed it towards Morag. 'There you are. Good Romanian pure methanol. It's a little sweet, I understand, but mixed with peatreek it is apparently delicious. And very potent.' Her expression hardened. 'Now drink!'

'I could tip it out.'

'Then it will be a bullet through your head instead. Now drink.'

Morag lifted the glass and took a sip.

'A proper drink. A good swig, Morag,' Helen ordered, holding the gun firmly in her hand.

Morag obeyed and grimaced. 'I don't like whisky at the best of times.'

'You'll find this rather strong, but soon you'll not care. It's quite moreish. That's what Robbie thought when he drank his peatreek that I added this to. He was a seasoned drinker and he loved it.'

'Were you his secret lover?'

Helen Beamish screwed up her face. 'I wouldn't exactly say I was his lover. I had sex with him, but there was no love involved. I had no choice.'

'I don't understand. You had regular sex with him?'

'Several times. Fairly kinky sex actually, but you don't really need to know the details. Suffice to say that I insisted on only two things. No kissing and always with a condom.' She waved the gun. 'Drink again. Another big swig.'

Morag acquiesced, feeling the liquid burn the back of her throat and give a warm sensation as it hit her stomach. She started to feel light-headed.

'I think if you had regular sex with him that makes you his lover?'

Helen shook her head impatiently. 'Of course it doesn't. The bastard was blackmailing me to sleep with him. He found out that I was syphoning off finances from some of the residents. He was quite shrewd actually. He worked out that I had been doing it for years, not just with them, but with lots of clients. All he wanted was for me to be his sex slave, so we would meet in his cabin, drink a little and have sex, however he liked it. He used to smirk and call me his dirty little secret, which I was. Then my actual lover started to get jealous.'

'Cameron, you mean?'

Helen laughed. 'Cameron! How ridiculous. We barely ever have sex.' She pointed at the glass. 'Finish it this time.'

Morag realised that her hand was starting to tremble. 'Will … will this kill me?'

Helen shrugged. 'Not straight away. But you'll soon pass out, just like Robbie did. Of course, he didn't know that I'd found where he had his peatreek delivered. The fool stored it outside in his old lobster pots. I obtained a good supply of methanol from my dear brother-in-law. You've no idea how simple it was to have it sent over to me. He was quite happy to let me have it from his lab, in exchange for sexual favours whenever I visit my sister.'

'You are a truly disgusting woman!'

Helen laughed and nodded. 'That may be true, but men seem to like that.' Lifting the bottle, she refilled the tumbler. 'Now drink.'

With a trembling hand Morag raised the glass and drank. She struggled to focus as her vision started to go slightly blurred. 'But the peatreek didn't kill Robbie, did it?'

'No. He was pretty drunk already, but after we had sex he drank more until he passed out. That was when I injected all of his insulin. Then I dragged him through from the bedroom, shoved a nasogastric tube down his throat and poured the rest of the peatreek down into his stomach. There was a bit of regurgitation and then he had a spectacular convulsion. He may have been dead from that, but I like to think it was when I smashed his face on the floor that he actually shuffled off his mortal coil. Then I cleared everything up.'

'Like his laptop and the used condom?'

'Of course. There was nothing on the laptop, but I couldn't risk it falling into anyone's hands.'

'And how did the teenagers get hold of it?'

'Ah, that was a mistake, I admit. I had doctored three bottles and left them in his lobster pot. One of the kids must have found one and taken it, I guess. Otherwise, I have no idea.'

'But when you heard about the teenagers at the pillbox you panicked?'

'Bloody right I did. That's why I sent lover-boy to search for Vicky Spiers. Fortunately, he found her and took her to one of our love-nests. We were planning on keeping her alive, just subdued with whisky until we decided where to take her and release her. Of course, that can't happen now. She's being terminated before we go.'

Morag gasped. 'You murderous bitch!'

'You just finish that drink. All of it this time.'

Morag raised the glass again. 'You'll never get away. This is an island and we'll block any route.'

'You mean you would if you were alive. Which right now is not looking likely.' Helen pointed the gun at the glass. 'Down the hatch. You know, you really shouldn't drink on duty. That's what they'll say when they find you after the road accident, when you drive over a cliff into the sea.'

Suddenly the door burst open and Cameron Beamish rushed in, a shotgun braced against his shoulder. 'You filthy cow! Put that gun down. You're even worse than I thought you were, but I've heard everything.'

Helen Beamish did not seem at all fazed. She continued to point the gun unwaveringly at Morag.

'Well, well, Cameron. Some gumption from you at last. I thought your little fling with Kathleen would be the limit of your capability, but here you are with your father's old Purdey. It hasn't been fired in thirty years, so put it down before you hurt yourself. You wouldn't have the nerve anyway.'

'Why, Helen?' he demanded. 'Why all this, when I gave you everything.'

She laughed. 'Because I hate you, you snivelling worm. I was going to leave you and let you see how you got on with that tart Kathleen, but I see that I'll have to —'

She spun round and fired, hitting him in the chest.

Cameron's body jolted backwards but he kept his feet. He lowered the shotgun and stared disbelievingly at the expanding patch of blood on his shirt. Then he staggered back against the wall and started to slide down.

Helen stepped towards him. 'You fool! You ruin everything. Now I'm going to have to make this look as if you lost your bottle and turned a shotgun on yourself. If only —'

She didn't finish for Morag launched herself at her, grasping her arm and slamming it down on the desk, causing the solicitor to scream in pain and release the gun. Morag followed it up with an elbow to her face that broke her nose and caused blood to gush from her nostrils.

But Morag's movements were slow and she was staggering after her exertion. Helen Beamish punched her in the face, causing her to fall back into the chair. Then Helen grabbed the gun and swivelled to point it at Morag's face.

'You interfering bloody —'

There was a sudden explosion and Helen was thrown across the room in a huge shower of blood as Cameron discharged both barrels of the Purdey.

Morag stared in horror at the mangled body, knowing that the woman was dead. She stood and turned to see Cameron's head slump down as he passed out, the shotgun falling across his lap. After staunching his wound as best she could she ran through into the sitting room and by the fireplace she shoved fingers down her throat to make herself sick. She heaved copious amounts into the empty fireplace and then pushed herself up and made for the side table upon which were several decanters of spirits.

'God, please make this work,' she muttered, pulling out the stopper from the whisky decanter and drinking mouthful after mouthful.

Staggering back to Helen Beamish's office with the decanter in one hand she felt for a pulse on what was left of Helen's body, but was unable to detect one. Picking up the telephone on the desk she called the station.

'Kyleshiffin Police Station,' came Calum Steele's voice. 'How may I help you? I'm afraid all of our officers are busy at the moment.'

'It's ... me, Calum,' she said, her voice heavily slurred. 'Is Torquil there?'

'No, it's just Cora and myself. It's — er — not been busy, but your Superintendent phoned. He wasn't too happy that I was left in charge. He said he'd have —'

'Never mind that, Calum. I ... need you to ring ... Doctor McLelland. And ring the others. I ... I need help. One death ... one badly wounded patient ... and me.'

'Where are you, Morag. I'll come myself.'

'At the ... Beamish house. You ... stay and mind ... the station. You're very special ... you and Cora...'

Morag hung up and took another hefty swig from the decanter before slumping into the chair and passing out.

Vicky swerved to her left, expecting the advancing figure to try to block her so that the man she was fleeing from could catch her. Together they would drag her back to that place and...

But the figure passed her and went straight for her pursuer. She stumbled through a puddle in her bare feet and slipped, landing on her face in the water. She pushed herself up and turned just in time to see the figure from the mist punch the other several times, causing him to fall down in a crumpled heap.

'It's all right, Vicky. It's me, Inspector McKinnon,' said the man, turning. 'Just stay there a moment while I handcuff this swine. Don't worry about him, he's out cold and can't hurt you.'

Scarcely believing that she was out of danger, Vicky sat up in time to see Torquil handcuffing the unconscious gallery owner, Nathan Westwood.

CHAPTER EIGHTEEN

'We are glad to see you out of hospital, Morag,' said Torquil as the West Uist team sat in the rest room the day after.

'I'm glad to be out, boss. I can't say that I like this hangover, though. Why people willingly drink vast amounts of whisky is beyond me.'

'You'll be pleased to hear that Catriona McDonald is being discharged home from the Western Isles Hospital today. Her vision is almost completely back.'

'What about Vicky? Her parents must be so relieved to have her home.'

'Ralph says he's going to arrange some counselling. She's probably still in shock, but post-traumatic stress syndrome is common after false imprisonment.'

'I can hardly believe that Helen Beamish could have been so evil,' Morag said. 'She had me fooled completely.'

'And she had everyone taken in, Morag,' Torquil replied. 'We've looked at the memory stick that Robbie Ochterlonie gave old Stuart Robertson for safe-keeping in case anything happened to him. It was inside one of his ships in bottles on his dressing table. She's been embezzling and exploiting clients right left and centre for years. She was the murderer all right, but she had her lover, Nathan Westwood, wrapped round her finger. They were stashing money away and he had no qualms about either imprisoning Vicky or indeed, killing her.'

Morag winced. 'That cold-blooded monster, Helen Beamish, said Vicky was being terminated while she tried to poison me. And if her poor husband hadn't come in when he did —'

'He knew that she was having an affair, but he wasn't sure with who,' said Torquil.

'I saw him on the moor on Monday morning,' Ewan volunteered. 'Wet weather gear and binoculars. He told me he was bird watching, but he must have been trying to spy on some of those cottages of theirs.'

'Poor man,' said Morag. 'I don't suppose he even knew about the embezzling. Will he be OK?'

'Yes, he was taken to the Western Isles Hospital and they flew a cardiothoracic surgeon in. She removed the bullet from his lung and resected it. He's in intensive care with IV lines and chest drains, but he's expected to recover physically. As for psychologically, after this, who knows.'

'Archie Reid is another one in shock,' Wallace said. 'He admitted that he'd been supplying Robbie Ochterlonie with peatreek for years, but was terrified that his peatreek could have been involved in either of the two events.'

'He had taken quite a beating from Angus Mackintosh,' added Douglas.

'How did Angus know that he supplied the peatreek?' Morag asked.

'Jamie Mackintosh kept a diary. We have it now. In it he made daily notes and it seemed he did all sorts of odd jobs around the island to make cash, including being Archie Reid's delivery boy. Clearly, he had taken one of the adulterated bottles of peatreek when he and Vicky and Catriona planned their celebration at the pillbox after their exams.'

Morag turned to Penny and Ewan, who were sitting side by side on the settee. She noted their thighs were touching and smiled to herself. They certainly seemed to have hit it off.

'What happened with Stan Wilkinson?' she asked.

'He was the burglar, Morag,' Ewan said. 'He wanted his phone back in case we found his pictures of him wearing all those stolen shoes.'

Penny explained that she had realised who he was, with the beard he had grown and his much shorter haircut. 'I think he's harmless enough. He just has this shoe fetish.'

'Aye, when he burgled the place he took all sorts of things to make it look as if it was random. The silly chap took the trainer and the other things from the search, not realising their importance. He said he couldn't resist my murder shoes.'

'Superintendent Lumsden took his officers back to Lewis,' Torquil continued. 'He was threatening all sorts of reprimands for leaving the station under the management of a civilian, but I sort of suggested that Calum could muster up quite a media storm against him, so all in all, I think it's going to be passed off, especially now that we have Vicky back. Of course, the Procurator Fiscal is going to open Fatal Accident Inquiries on the deaths of Jamie Mackintosh, Robbie Ochterlonie and now Helen Beamish. We're going to be busy. Also, since Calum's last bulletin all sorts of things have come out of the woodwork.'

'Such as?' Morag asked.

'Well, sexual shenanigans for starters. The Corlin-MacLeods are splitting up, because Esther has been having an affair with Councillor Charlie McDonald. Apparently he had taken solace in golf and the Padre has acquired a new parishioner. Hamish McNab has also been a bad lad and has been using his mistress, Doreen McGuire to spy on McDonald's daughter and gain whatever dirt she could about Charlie. There are financial irregularities and unscrupulous behaviour over properties and licensing to be investigated.'

The bell from the front door rang and Ewan leaped to his feet to go through to see who had come in.

A moment later he came back in. 'Look who's here.'

The Padre walked in with a beaming smile. 'No, he didn't mean me. She wanted to surprise you so she called me to pick her up from the ferry on the Ariel.'

Lorna walked in and went straight to Torquil and they exchanged polite air kisses, knowing that they would exchange them for the real thing once they were alone.

'Superintendent Lumsden sent me over. He said you'd need some help picking all the pieces up. He almost seemed human.' From a shoulder bag she drew out a bottle. 'Look what he sent for the wedding guests to enjoy at the wedding. It's a 50-year-old malt whisky. A good one from Cambeltown.'

'Whisky!' Torquil said. 'Look, about that, Lorna, I've been thinking. I'm not so sure that whisky would be right for the wedding favours.'

'Oh, that's a change of heart. And what about that other question. Have you decided?'

Torquil grinned. He knew she was referring to his choice for best man. 'Actually, I have. There are going to be five of them!'

A NOTE TO THE READER

Dear Reader,

Thank you for taking the time to read my novel, I hope that you enjoyed reading about the dark things that can happen on my idyllic little Scottish island on the edge of the world.

It is true that characters in a novel often take on a life of their own. That happened several times in this novel, when the story did not follow the path that I had imagined it would take. The characters felt so at home on the island of West Uist that they felt empowered to pay the piper to play their macabre tune.

I have been a lifelong fan of crime fiction, but to my mind the use of the laboratory and the revelations that DNA testing can instantly give, somehow rob many modern crime novels of their sense of romance. That was why I set my story on the remote Hebridean island of West Uist, so that it would be far removed from the modern forensic crime thriller. Also, because the island has the smallest police force in the country, it would not another gritty, urban police procedural. Crimes would have to be solved in a very old-fashioned manner.

I studied medicine at the University of Dundee and did some of my training in the highlands. I loved the sense of community in villages and determined that if I ever wrote a crime novel it would feature a Scottish detective working in a remote place, aided by friends, family and the local newspaper. Years later when Inspector Torquil McKinnon walked into my imagination I set about learning to play the bagpipes, although unlike Torquil, the winner of the Silver Quaich I have never been anything other than dire. Nonetheless, playing around with my pipes helps me as I am working out my plots.

Since golf is also a hobby and I had played on the remotest Hebridean courses, those sheep-nibbled links complete with dive bombing gulls had to appear in the stories. When I venture onto my local golf course I imagine the Padre, a steady 8 handicapper, playing alongside me, advising me on how to hit the green, sink a putt – or solve the newest clue.

If you have enjoyed the novel enough to leave a review on **Amazon** and **Goodreads**, then I would be truly grateful.

Keith Moray

https://keithmorayauthor.com

Sapere Books is an exciting new publisher of brilliant fiction and popular history.

To find out more about our latest releases and our monthly bargain books visit our website:
saperebooks.com